Braids
Take a
Day

ZAINAB BOLADALE is a journalist, television presenter and public speaker. She was born in Nigeria and raised in Ireland. In 2017, she made her TV debut on RTÉ's children's programme, *news2day*, as the first Afro-Irish woman on Irish TV news. On *news2day*, she presented stories from around the world to the young people of Ireland. Zainab now travels around the country as a presenter and reporter for Ireland's long-running factual feature programme, *Nationwide*. Zainab has also written and directed her first short film, *Worthy*, released in 2023. This is her first book. You can find out more about Zainab on Boladale.com.

ZAINAB BOLADALE

THE O'BRIEN PRESS
DUBLIN

This edition first published 2024 by
The O'Brien Press Ltd,
12 Terenure Road East, Rathgar,
Dublin 6, D06 HD27, Ireland.
Tel: +353 1 4923333; Fax: +353 1 4922777
E-mail: books@obrien.ie
Website: obrien.ie

The O'Brien Press is a member of Publishing Ireland
ISBN: 978-1-78849-442-7
Text © copyright Zainab Boladale 2024
The moral rights of the author have been asserted.
Copyright for typesetting, layout, editing, design
© The O'Brien Press Ltd
Layout and design by Emma Byrne
Cover illustration by Grace Enemaku
Author photograph: Courtesy of RTÉ Archives; used with permission.

1 3 5 7 9 8 6 4 2
24 26 28 27 25

Printed and bound by Nørhaven Paperback A/S, Denmark.

Published in
DUBLIN
UNESCO
City of Literature

Enjoying life with
O'BRIEN
obrien.ie

MIX
Paper | Supporting
responsible forestry
FSC® C104608
FSC
www.fsc.org

The O'Brien Press received financial assistance
from the Arts Council to publish this title

CONTENTS

CHAPTER ONE

FAREWELL, ST ENDA'S

The pages in front of me were covered in all the history notes I had crammed into my brain over the past few weeks. This was my final exam, and in these last two hours I'd been gripping my pen so tightly that my fingers felt stiff, and my wrist ached. I stretched both hands over my table to give them a sense of relief.

This classroom, which our sixth-year teachers normally used to gather us for attendance and uniform checks, was far emptier than it had been in our English Paper One exam, last Wednesday. I quietly did a head count; there were thirteen of us in total. Eight students were still writing.

The Callaghan brothers were both bent over their desks, scribbling away like their lives depended on answering each question. Just that morning they'd been boasting about how little they needed to study since they had gotten H1s in their mock exams months before, but now from the redness and sweat on their faces, I wondered if they might have under-estimated how different the 'real' exam questions could be.

The whole room felt tense, you could almost touch the stress in the air. Marie-Clare, the girl I shared the most classes with, had also finished with her exam paper. She had her pages neatly piled on top of each other and her pens and pencils lined up across the table.

Marie-Clare was one of those people who soaked every bit of information in like she was a sponge. I liked that she was always so excited to help others; it didn't come as a surprise when she told me during Maths class one day that she wanted to be a teacher. She was the class prefect, and had won a 'Best Student' award last year, so it seemed fitting.

The two students beside her, Dara and Josephine, looked anxious, as though they weren't sure if anything they had written was correct. Their eyes kept darting from the wall clock at the top of the room to the pages they were flipping through.

I could see the back of Sinéad's head, her straight black hair in a low bun. She was sitting sideways, her elbow on the table and her face pressed into the palm of her hand. She seemed tired and fed up, and honestly, I wasn't far off feeling the same.

The woman in charge of supervising our exam looked just as tired as I felt. I wondered how much she would get paid for making sure we didn't cheat. To me, her job seemed simple enough. I glanced up at the clock behind her, our eyes met and as if she could read my mind, she too turned around to look.

'You can now stop writing,' she announced. 'Organise your answer sheets and remain in your seats until I've collected them all!'

This was the moment I had been waiting for.

A collective sigh of relief filled the room. I sank back into my chair, finally able to let go of the mountain of tension that had been building up all week. There is only so much studying and preparation a girl can do, but finally, this was it. The end of my last exam and hopefully nothing would stress me out this much for the rest of the summer.

It felt strange that my time at secondary school was finally over. I didn't hate St Enda's, but the thought of no longer rushing down these locker-lined corridors to reach my 9am classes filled me with joy.

With around a hundred and eighty students in total, it's a small school: you've got the farm kids, the townies and the blow-ins. Even if we don't all talk to each other, we all know – or at least recognise – each other. While that sometimes has its perks, it also means there's no escaping the watchful eye of the teachers and the daily rumour mills.

'Are you well!' Sinéad screamed as soon as she spotted me amongst the crowd of maroon-uniformed students walking out of our red-brick school building.

Sixth-year students were now pouring out of the school's heavy wooden doors and forming their friend circles. Some had come from history, like me. Others had sat their French exam earlier in the day. I tried to read their faces; some were happy and others looked worried about what they'd just left behind on those once blank pages.

I was finished! Others, like Marie-Clare and the Callaghan brothers, still had to sit Technology and Religious Education next week. They were heading in the direction of the school library, a separate building just beside the main one. Unfortunately for them, their misery wasn't over yet. I waved at Marie-Clare as though I was sending some comfort her way and she waved back.

The school car park was just as busy with many anxious parents waiting. I skipped toward my best friend, holding my arms out to give her a big hug. 'Sinéad, I can't believe we're really done,' I said, smiling, 'we're actually free.'

I started to tell her about the history questions I found easy and the ones that surprised me.

'Abi, the LAST thing I want to talk about is this night-mare we've had to go through,' Sinéad said scoldingly mid-embrace. She hated that I cared so much about these exams and in turn, I wished she cared more. I knew it didn't determine our entire lives, but I still wanted to look back and be proud of how I did in school, even if no one ever asks about it.

'Let's focus on the important things,' said Sinéad, shaking me as though it would help her words sink in better. 'We're about to have the very BEST summer of our lives!'

Mrs McGann, our now-former Maths teacher, was watching us from the school gate and motioning for us to leave. Her face was all scrunched up; students joked that it was probably from her constant frowning.

'Let's go, let's go…' I said, forgetting that neither she nor our other teachers had any power over us now. Sinéad stuck her tongue and middle finger out at Mrs McGann, then pulled me by my jumper as she ran off, forcing me to do the same.

It was less than a ten-minute walk to Vinny's Takeaway, also known as 'our local chipper'. This was the hangout spot for many of us in Ennistymon. We loved it here because you could get a decent feed for good value.

There wasn't a lot going on for us teens here outside of the summer months. If you were lucky enough to be friends

11

with someone who could drive, then you'd have the option of going into another nearby town or village.

Around here, the most exciting calendar event was Electric, the monthly teenage disco that took place in Ennis town. It had always puzzled me how even students without cars would somehow find a ride there and back in the late hours of the night. The girls at St Enda's would spend their lunch breaks gossiping about what went down on the dance floor, who kissed who and what drinks they snuck in.

The rest of us who couldn't go would pretend to be too cool to care about something as frivolous as a disco. We cared, but some of us just had strict parents who were unwilling to hear us out.

I'm talking about myself.

The reason I knew I would never be allowed to go all boiled down to my dad; he had always made it clear that he felt that teenagers shouldn't have interesting lives outside of school. Even though I disagreed, being able to say, 'Sorry, my dad is kind of strict,' when I'd get invited for late night parties or sleepovers at parent-free houses saved me from a lot of things I didn't feel I was prepared for. Especially after hearing the stories of what 'scandalous' activities went down.

Out of curiosity, though, I tried to suggest going to Electric as a reward for good grades last year, but as expected, he snickered and said, 'Abidemi, the days for parties will come, but not while you're in this house!'

After that shut-down, I never bothered to bring it up again.

Sinéad couldn't go either. Her oldest sister Margaret, who used to always go out, even to discos as far out as Limerick city, got pregnant before finishing her final year at St Enda's. As a result, Sinéad's mom, who herself had Margaret before finishing school, got stricter with the younger two sisters.

When we finally arrived at Vinny's, we made our way to the counter and ordered two burgers and chips to share.

'Nine euro please,' said the man behind the till. Perhaps it was part of his look, but he always managed to have grease stains on his shirt and beads of sweat pooled around his wrinkled forehead. He was Vinny, the owner of the takeaway.

Behind Vinny was Jack Keane. Although he was in my French and Maths class at St Enda's we never really talked at school. He had his own group of friends, mainly the football-obsessed lads whose yearly goal was to make the county finals in their sports clubs, but I'd never seen Jack share the same excitement with them. I'd always wondered if they were really his core friend-group or was it the case that he hung out with them because they all grew up together.

I also didn't know for sure if Jack was Vinny's son or if they were related. I had only ever seen Jack's mom at parent-teacher events over the years.

Jack and Vinny didn't look alike, but they both seemed to have the same sense of humour. They were loudly sarcastic when giving out to each other and Jack never had any fear of being fired.

Today, it was Jack in the kitchen, which was separated by a thin metal shelf that held all the freshly cooked meals waiting to be assembled. He was dancing between the sizzling fryer and a line of hamburger meat, which he carefully flipped while they grilled.

Sometimes, when he was up front and working the till, he would fill the brown chip bags right up to the top, and he didn't go light on the free sauces he handed out! He was nice to us and always greeted us by name.

While watching Jack work, I wondered if he had finished with all of his Leaving Cert exams. I wanted to know if he too was 'free from St Enda's', but I felt too nervous to ask, so as usual, I left the talking to Sinéad.

'Hi, Jack,' Sinéad shouted, waving at him from where we stood. He lifted his head and flashed us a smile; his hands were focused on shaking dripping oil out of a basket of freshly fried chips.

We took our seat at a corner booth, the one we had etched our names into some years ago. Here at Vinny's, we were able to escape into our own little world.

'Right so, Abi, we need to figure out our plans for this

summer,' said Sinéad matter-of-factly, while pouring salt and vinegar over the chips.

'What do you mean?' I said, sinking my teeth into my burger. I savoured it for a few seconds before continuing, 'I thought we were just going to take it easy all summer.'

Sinéad rolled her eyes and pulled out her phone. She typed in a few letters before pushing the screen right up to my face, making me jerk back a little. On her screen was an Instagram post from Electric nightclub in Ennis town. On a terribly designed neon graphic poster were the details of their next event.

'*SUMMER TUNES with DJ Cheez, July 1st. Tickets €20.*'

'Oh…' I said slowly, finally getting what she was suggesting. Was she crazy? This event was only a week away.

'No, no, no, Sinéad, my dad AND your mom would kill us!' I said, shaking my head.

'Girl, don't be such a bore-bag! We're grown now, you're about to be an eighteen-year-old woman, you're graduating from girlhood, so you've got to start acting like it!'

Sinéad's words stung a little bit because I felt nothing like a soon-to-be-woman. Unlike most of the girls at St Enda's, I'd never had a boyfriend, never had my first kiss, I wore the same style of clothes I did when I was thirteen and I didn't have a 'beauty routine' like some of the other girls. The idea of officially being a 'woman' felt like a distant concept to me and my experiences.

Sinéad could see me getting lost in my thoughts, so she poked the dimple in my cheek to draw me back to her. 'Anyway, I'm just saying … everyone knows asking for forgiveness is better than asking for permission,' Sinéad said, smiling at me, her mischievous green eyes waiting for me to take the bait.

I knew this routine all over. Sinéad would suggest something we shouldn't be doing, and I'd go along with it while praying to all the patron saints in heaven that we wouldn't get in trouble for it.

'Just have a think about it,' Sinéad said, pulling at one of my braids. 'I just want to make memories with you before you leave me and go off to Trinity College. You might come back thinking you're too good to be my friend.' She said it jokingly, but I knew she really felt that way.

The thing is, our friendship began when we were nine years old, I think we were in third class at the time. In those days, Sinéad and her cousins were stuck together like glue. It didn't matter that they were in separate classes, several years apart.

It wasn't until her cousins finished primary school, leaving her to spend most of her break times alone, that our classmates – me included – really noticed Sinéad.

This was when the bullying started.

The boys in our class decided to nickname her 'soap girl' because she very often came into school smelling like the strongest lavender soap, which was good, until it wasn't. The scent would fill up the whole classroom to the point that some of us would start sneezing and the teacher would have to open the windows.

One afternoon, I asked her if she wanted to sit beside me since my desk was right next to the window. Ever since then, we've never been apart for too long.

I guess Sinéad was also now thinking about the fact that after this summer, for the first time since our friendship began, we would no longer have the comfort of being together, almost every single day, especially during the school term.

Assuming all went well with our exams, I'd be moving to Dublin to study this September. Sinéad, on the other hand, didn't know if she wanted to study. She loved art, but I guess she didn't feel strongly enough about it to pursue it any further. I didn't want to press her too much about it either.

For now, her plan was to work at her mom's launderette till she could figure it all out. Whenever I tried to ask her about what she would like to study, she'd always change the subject.

When we were all asked to fill out our college application form, I asked her if she wanted help filling hers, but she ignored me, so I didn't push her further.

She'd never admit it, but I felt she'd be good at something art related – after all, her portfolio was the one thing I had ever seen her pour all her energy into. She loved to draw comic-book style characters during our lunch breaks, and I could see her becoming an illustrator one day.

I wanted to experience going to a Dublin college *with* Sinéad, that way we could live the big city life together, but she said she wasn't keen on the idea.

'Why would I be bothered!' she once said, putting an end to the topic there and then.

Now, as for the disco she was pushing for us to go to, I decided it'd be best to give her an answer that I didn't have to commit to. Sinéad already knew what my dad was like; he just wouldn't get it.

'OK, I'll consider it … but, like, you know … the way my dad is …' I responded in hopes that she would understand this to be a subtle 'no'.

'We'll come up with a plan,' Sinéad said, swinging her arm around my shoulder to give me a sideways hug as though she had somehow heard a 'yes' in my words.

From the corner of my eye, I noticed that Jack was now out of the kitchen and wiping down the tables around us. I wondered what his plans were for the summer.

How did the exams go for him? Did he care much about school? Was he planning to go to college? Here at Vinny's,

Jack didn't talk about school, so it was hard to know how he felt about it all.

Watching Jack move around, I could see why many of the girls at St Enda's found him handsome. He hadn't been a 'boyfriend' to any of them and I always wondered why, since they all crushed on him. Jack was tall with broad shoulders and moved with a lot of confidence. He was very likeable and gentle. He also managed to do a decent job of staying out of the gossip train that ran through our school.

Jack must have felt me staring at him; he turned his head, causing his thick brown hair to flop around his face.

'All good with you, Abi?' he asked.

I felt an instant wave of panic rush through me. Without thinking, I pushed the last bite of my burger into my mouth and forced a half smile. I nodded while pointing to my full mouth, implying I couldn't possibly talk back.

Jack chuckled softly to himself and gave me a nod of understanding before returning to clean the tables beside us.

'Not like you to be stuck for words, huh, Abi?' Sinéad said, raising her eyebrow at me while looking a little too amused. She grabbed a tissue to clean up the burger sauce that had smeared itself on the side of my lips.

UGGGH, I'm such a fool! I thought to myself. It must have looked like I was pointing to the clump of burger sauce on my lip. I felt so embarrassed that I found myself praying for the ground to swallow me up immediately.

To save myself from any more awkward interactions, all I could do was sink lower into my seat and wish to be granted the kind of superpowers that would let me rewind these last few cringeworthy seconds.

CHAPTER TWO

FREEDOM AT LAST

The sun was still casting a warm glow over our town when we finally decided to leave Vinny's that evening.

In the winter months, the walk back home could be horrible, but in the height of the summer it was beyond heavenly.

The main street was lined with traditional-looking Irish shops and hidden behind them, you could hear the unmistakable sounds of the River Inagh trickling down into the Cascades waterfall. Things I considered boring seemed to be other people's tourist attractions. Traffic ran through the town as people poured in from picturesque Doolin or the beach town of Lahinch.

To get back home, I had to cross a small stone bridge and go up a little hill. I'd follow that road, passing rows of mismatched houses. They seemed to be a history lesson on what style of building was trendy in the years they were built.

As I went further up the hill, it got greener and some of the houses got bigger, more country in style. Some had low stone walls marking off the land around them and the front yard displayed a mix of wildflowers in all sorts of colours – purples, yellows and whites. I sometimes felt tempted to pick them during my walk.

I could spot my house from afar, thanks to Dad's SUV chilling out in front. Our place was a renovated two-storey country house passed down from Mom's side of the family. It sat on top of the hill. If the sky was clear, on a good day like today from its upstairs windows you could see long stretches of vivid green land, pops of colourful flora and the waves of the Atlantic Ocean shimmering in the distance.

Mom's entire family lived here at one point; it was her childhood home. When her parents realised they no longer needed such a big place once all their children got married, they decided to put it on the market and moved to Wicklow. I had visited them when I was much younger.

That move happened during the Irish recession when downsizing was what everybody was doing. Not Mom and Dad – they were on the house-hunting train and ended up buying it. The first thing Mom did was paint the front door this vibrant seaside blue – her favourite colour.

I was around seven years old when cancer started to reveal its ugly face and chip away at Mom's health, right up until her passing. Sometimes, I feel like the memories I have from that time belong to someone else, that's how distant it all feels now.

Back then, Mom would excitedly tell me stories of how she and Dad first crossed paths on campus at Trinity College. She was all about becoming a teacher, while he was diving into the world of accounting; both were very academic and would always bump into each other in the library. It was one of the reasons Dad was eager for me to attend Trinity. 'It can be our family tradition,' he'd say with a grin.

Dad's upbringing was very different to Mom's. He talked less about it, but from the times he did share, I knew that he was born in Ekiti state, Nigeria. The first time he boarded a flight was after winning a fully funded international scholarship. This opportunity would have landed him anywhere in Europe – sunny places like Portugal, Italy or Spain, but he chose good old rainy Ireland. He said it was because he knew a bit about Ireland because of the friendly Irish nuns who used to pop into his boarding school on mission trips.

As I walked through the door, I could hear Dad's voice in the kitchen; he sounded like he was on the phone.

'The new clients don't want to see the report, so it doesn't make sense for us to rush it, *naa big waste of resource be that.*' Dad sounded frustrated, and I could tell from his pidgin English – often spoken between Nigerians who don't share one of the many local languages – that he was talking to a Nigerian colleague.

Closing the door behind me, I kicked off my black school trainers and slipped into my comfy grey fluffy slippers, neatly lined up on the shoe rack by the entrance.

The shoe rack was actually a Christmas present from Anne, our cleaner. She wasn't too thrilled with the idea of us stomping around in outdoor shoes inside. All our floors were hardwood, and she'd often comment on how much dirt we seemed to bring inside. 'You've practically brought the whole earth in here!' she'd say grumpily.

Unlike Dad, I took the correction and immediately got him to order us the house slippers I'm now wearing. We got them that same week, but he still hasn't taken his pair out of the plastic wrapping. Even now, he was pacing around the kitchen in his black leather lace-up shoes.

As I settled in, Dad was still on the phone, though slightly muffled. He seemed to be having a heated argument. 'My daughter is back, let's continue this later,' he said, his tone suggesting a bit of annoyance with the person on the other end of the line.

In his late twenties, Dad used to work as an independent accountant, with a list of small clients that essentially made him his own boss. Then, up until last year, he was employed as an accountant for an Irish tech company based in Limerick. He often joked that it was run by 'men with fragile egos'. I think he just didn't like being told what to do.

That job meant Dad got a fixed monthly pay with enough benefits to meet our needs, but that wasn't why he took it in the first place. After Mom was diagnosed, he needed something stable and close to the hospital.

He never planned to stay at the tech company for six years, but after we lost Mom, staying in that job was one less change in his life and that brought him some comfort.

That all changed two years ago when Dad made a trip to Nigeria for his boarding school reunion. Having never been to Nigeria, I begged to go with him, but Dad wouldn't let me. I was so annoyed. I mean, why tell me stories about Nigerian culture and Yoruba customs, but not let me experience it for myself, especially after all these years?

During that trip, Dad reconnected with an old friend, Balogun, who had inherited one of his father's companies. 'Under The Sun' was a major food brand that specialised in African food products. They exported to many countries, including to African stores in Ireland.

Balogun mentioned that he was looking for some new accountants, especially ones who had 'international' education. When Dad returned home from that trip, he was beyond thrilled. Over dinner one night, he told me that he hoped to get the job even though it meant being away a lot on business trips, but the impressive salary made it all the more attractive.

'I am indeed a lucky man,' he said when Balogun later confirmed the job was his, he didn't even have to interview for it!

Dad later told me that his plan was to buy a home in Nigeria for me to comfortably visit and finally meet his side of the family who I had only ever talked to on the phone. In the meantime, he would bring back little gifts for me from his mother who he said couldn't wait to meet her namesake. This was exciting!

Dad's new job was demanding, but it brought about a noticeable change in him – it made him happier, he joked around a lot more. He was also very generous with the pocket money he'd give me. The €10 that I'd grown used to stretching across one week quickly turned to €30 and for the first time in my life, I had money that I didn't know what to spend on. So, I just started to save it all in a little tin box. I figured I'd need it more when I'm off to college.

'Is it going to be a results sheet full of H1s?' Dad teased, sliding his phone into his back pocket as I walked into the kitchen. 'How did the exam go today? Did you write an answer for every question?'

'I don't know about H1s, but I feel good about it all,' I said, smiling back at him, not committing myself to his expectations of excellence.

I grabbed a stool from the kitchen island and plopped down on it, letting my schoolbag drop to the floor beside me. Dad had stopped his pacing and now stood across from me, his arms folded.

Physically, Dad wasn't bulky, but he had a solid build and was quite tall, giving him a strong presence. He kept his coarse hair trimmed close and his bristly moustache hovered above his lips like a little cap. In a different world, he might have made a good army general; he had that 'no-nonsense' aura about him. Few people would guess that underneath that exterior, he had his softer moments too.

'Don't you know that you have your dad's genius brain, so I already know you did a good job on those papers!' he said.

Ignoring his playful comment, I was now eyeing up a glossy pink envelope on the kitchen counter. He saw that I had noticed it.

'Oh, that thing. I meant to leave it on your bed, but since you've seen it now, you might as well open it. It's like the end of your secondary school adventure ...' he trailed off, a nostalgic smile forming on his lips. I could see him lost in memories of the past, probably thinking of the day he first sent me off to school in a well-ironed uniform.

Inside the envelope was a white card; it had confetti drawn all over it and in bubbly balloon-like writing it read 'YOU DID IT.' A generic message to mark whatever congratulatory occasion fitted.

Within the wide card was a folded fifty-euro note and a handwritten message: '*Abidemi, your parents are deeply proud of the young woman you're becoming, may your light always shine bright.*'

A soft silence hung between us, filled with unspoken emotions. This was a special moment with a bitter-sweet truth; Mom was there for my first day of school and should have been part of my last. Sadly, life had its own plans. Dad and I realised some time ago that talking about her brought more hurt than comfort. So, in times like this, we allowed ourselves to pretend she was still with us, also marking our celebrations.

'Would you like me to go pick up a pizza from Lahinch?' Dad said, breaking the silence and changing the mood; he wasn't one to dwell on things for too long.

'I had food with Sinéad at Vinny's,' I replied, thinking about my earlier conversation. Would I have a chance to ask about the disco now? Dad wouldn't be able to argue that I needed to focus on school since that was all done!

Unfortunately, his phone interrupted my thoughts and what could have been good timing. Taking the phone back out of his pocket, he stared at the caller ID while cursing under his breath. 'Why would you call me at this time?' he said in frustration.

'Abi, since you're almost an adult now … can I trust you to take care of the house?' He paused, trying to read my reaction as though he was expecting me to be surprised. It wasn't the first time he'd been away for work, so I was slightly puzzled by the seriousness in his tone.

'Yes, of course!' I replied confidently.

'I know it's a lot, but I'll be gone for three weeks this time!' he continued, his brows furrowing as he spoke. 'I have to prepare a financial plan for the coming year, and they insist on examining the documents in person, considering their sensitivity.'

THREE WEEKS. THREE WHOLE SUMMER WEEKS. I couldn't believe my luck.

It took everything in me not to smile from ear to ear.

'Oh,' I said, pretending to be a little upset. After all, this was the longest amount of time he'd ever been away from home because of work, but then a thought popped in. 'Am I staying with Ms Kelly then?' I asked, trying to hide the potential disappointment in my voice.

Ms Kelly lived in the small cottage just beside us on the hill with her two cats and a yard full of chickens. She was much older than Mom and Dad, but she liked them, and they got on really well. They had a neighbourly friendship between them.

Ms Kelly was as sharp as a whistle and kept herself busy. She spent most of her days tending to the land around her or selling her chicken's eggs, homemade jams and honey from her bees in local shops and to the ladies in her church.

Ms Kelly's roots in the community ran deep; she could effortlessly trace any local family's connections with just a few details. She had witnessed the evolution of Ennistymon and, more interestingly, of Ireland itself.

While I wasn't sure if she'd ever considered having children of her own, she often referred to herself as my 'third grandma'. Over the years, Ms Kelly had been the go-to babysitter whenever Dad needed to be away.

'I think you'd be able to handle three weeks on your own by now,' Dad said. 'You've been fine all the other times I've been away.'

Dad's tone changed again; he was back to his strict parent mode. 'Just make sure that Sinéad is the only person that you have over.' I could clearly read between the lines; this was his way of saying 'No BOYS allowed.'

Dad never asked me about boys, let alone boyfriends, but he'd always found ways to show his disapproval, like when Ms Kelly had her twenty-year-old nephew visit from London for a couple of days last December.

They had come over for lunch and Ms Kelly suggested to Dad that maybe I could bring him to the local Christmas Market so he could pick up a few presents to bring back to his family in London. Dad's response was, 'She's too busy preparing for her Christmas test.' This was a lie because by 18 December, they were well and truly over.

'Anyway, Ms Kelly will come here occasionally to check that you're OK and I've told her to let me know if she sees anything suspicious!' Dad said. 'You can tell Sinéad that too.'

Dad had a way of seeing through Sinéad's innocent act whenever she came over. He liked her, but he was aware that she had a bit more of a rebellious streak than I did. Despite that, he was glad to know that I had her as a friend.

A sense of relief washed over me. Was this what freedom felt like? This was a *big* step. It was a new level of trust and independence that I was eager to embrace.

CHAPTER THREE

FINDING BEAUTY

Our Saturday routine was always the same. Dad would do the 'big shop' to stock up on fresh ingredients and Anne would come for the 'big clean' around the house.

The main reason I enjoyed tagging along with Dad was so I could make sure he bought enough snacks and sweets, but as I got older, I started to understand that the 'big shop' wasn't just about groceries; it was an opportunity for Dad to chat with local shopkeepers and exchange friendly banter. Dad was just keeping up with local news, the kind that you could only find out through word of mouth.

Most locals recognised Dad, and while he never told them much about himself, they'd ask him to come to town meetings or join the community groups trying to make a difference in the area. They even once tried to get Dad to volunteer to be part of the 'Tidy Towns' clean-up crew, which most definitely wasn't his thing, but if someone was selling raffle tickets to raise money or a petition needed signing, they knew they could ask Dad for support. His weekends in town gave him a chance to connect, to be a part of the town's pulse, and to contribute in his own quiet way.

This Saturday though, I had my own plans. Finally able to relax again now that I no longer had exams to study for, I had the time to change up my hair.

My hair has always been naturally thick with curls that just about reach my shoulders. For the last six weeks, though, I've been wearing it in braids. Some of them have already come undone as the new growth at the roots made them looser.

Three years ago, I decided to start braiding my own hair. This came after a string of bad experiences with hairdressers who didn't understand how to handle my curls.

They'd suggest straightening it, sometimes with harsh chemicals, so they could 'manage' it better. I'd watch as the flat-iron passed over my curls, leaving behind stiff hair strands and the smell of heat and products in the air. They'd then pull and cut my hair, grinning nervously at me in the mirror while I watched their every move.

Leaving the salon, my hair would look great, my once voluminous curls hanging straight down like curtains. By the end of the week, though, my stubborn curls would bounce back in a weakened and straw-like state.

After I had spent years dealing with the damage and keeping my hair up in a bun to hide it, Dad eventually took me to a place called 'Shaba.' It was a Black hair salon he found in Limerick city. The shop was a colourful den filled with a selection of products, hair extensions and wigs, stacked from floor to ceiling. Most of the packaging featured smiling women with different skin tones and hair textures, which was a promising sign.

The owner of the shop was a vibrantly dressed Ghanaian woman called Abina, but everyone called her 'Auntie'. The first time we went, Dad guided me toward her, and as if she'd been expecting us, she pulled out a big black chair and tapped on it, signalling for me to sit down.

'Don't worry, girl, I'll make you beautiful,' she said, drawing out each word like a song, her smile widening to reveal a shiny gold front tooth.

She tightly braided rows of neat plaits across my head, but it was as if she forgot that my hair was attached to my scalp! When she folded my curl into the straight black hair extension she held, I couldn't help but whimper in pain.

'Don't move, you'll spoil the hair!' she said, pushing my fingers away as I reached to soothe my suffering scalp. 'You're too tender-headed!' She finished off a braid only to painfully plant a fresh new row while I silently fought back tears.

Three hours later she declared she was done. She grabbed

a cup full of hot water that another worker had prepared for her and a kitchen towel. She soaked the towel in the hot water and repeatedly use it to balm my scalp, her hands numb to the heat. 'To ease the tension,' she explained as I stared at her in confusion.

'Your daughter is so pretty now,' she told Dad, who'd been tapping away at his phone, probably replying to work emails, oblivious to the drama of my transformation. 'Don't go anywhere else, OK? My job is the best around,' she said, while tucking the money Dad gave her in a pouch tied around her waist, handing me back like a revamped piece of furniture.

Despite all the pain it took to put them in, I really did feel pretty the first time I saw my hair in braids. After several more visits to Shaba's Black hair salon, I decided that I would teach myself to braid my own hair!

By midday, I had finished undoing the last braid with the help of a rat-tail comb, its pointed metal end easing through the stubborn knots. It was the distant hum of a car engine that broke my concentration. Glancing out the window, I spotted Anne's car pulling out of our driveway.

Dad hadn't returned home yet and all the ingredients in the house required some real cooking. I decided to skip lunch and move on to washing my hair.

Stepping into the shower, I let the water flow through my tangled curls, gradually working to detangle them. After going through the repetitive motion of applying generous amounts of shampoo and conditioner, then rinsing it out, I wrapped my hair in an old cotton t-shirt to soak up the excess water that was dripping around me.

All the knowledge I've gained about caring for my hair has come from YouTube. I've spent years watching tutorial videos created by Black women who make the process of transforming their hair look so easy. The way they talk about their hair helps me appreciate my own.

Even now as I lather a layer of leave-in conditioner into my hair, it feels like I'm making up for the years when I so needed haircare.

Once in my room, I gathered my bag of hair tools that I'd need within arm's reach. Sitting cross-legged on my bed with my back to the window, I reached for my laptop and perched it on my bedside table, so it faced me.

My most recent YouTube search tab was still open: 'How to do Fulani Braids'.

Scrolling through all the results, I selected the video titled: 'Hair by Stacy – Fulani Braids.' Stacy, with her distinct American accent and her natural afro proudly on display, smiled at me from the screen. She began carefully explaining the unique features of Fulani braids.

'So, you want to do Fulani braids? Well, you should know that it's a traditional West African tribal style,' she explained on the video. 'They're usually recognised by a centre corn-row that runs from the forehead to the back of your neck. Smaller horizontal braids are then woven around the central braid, creating a delicate and intricate look. This hairstyle has been worn for centuries and holds cultural significance to certain tribes. Nowadays, this hairstyle is worn by Black women around the world.'

She finished her explanation and began demonstrating how to start using her own hair. 'Divide your hair in three sections ....' she instructed, while going on to talk about the importance of creating a good braiding foundation.

I copied her exact movements and picked up a small section of my own shoulder-length hair, along with the smallest amount of silky braiding hair extension. I began to weave it in, passing it from one hand to the other. It took a couple of tries before I got the hang of it. My braiding technique was still very weak compared to Stacy's.

The extensions, which Dad would buy in bulk for me from Shaba's hair salon, would add some thickness to my own hair. These extensions were pre-stretched, meaning the end of each strand was already tapered out. I didn't have to worry about the ends of my braids having a natural finish, so this was one less thing for me to think about. I didn't have to do much work. From my roots, once braided in, these extensions would stretch down to my lower back.

I got so lost in the process that I didn't hear Dad calling for me to come downstairs when he returned from the big shop. My dedication to my tranformation was disturbed by his heavy footsteps approaching my room.

He pushed the door open and looked at me in surprise. 'This one is new, but I think I've seen it on my younger sister before,' he said.

'It's called Fulani braids!' I said, eager to tell him everything I had learned about it.

'Oh, really? I didn't know there was a name for it,' Dad said. 'I don't know about you but I'm hungry. I'm making jollof rice and chicken, come downstairs when you're ready.'

I hadn't noticed that the room had grown darker as the sun had set outside. Dad turned on the light before leaving the room, giving me a gentle reminder that it would soon be dinner time. I only had a few braids left so I challenged myself to finish in the next thirty minutes. The race against time was on as my fingers moved quickly. Even the simplest braided hairstyle can take a couple of hours and for someone who's just learning and ambitious about the type of braids I want, they really do take a day!

Section. Weave. Braid. Repeat.

Section. Weave. Braid. Repeat.

Section. Weave. Braid.

Finally, I was finished!

CHAPTER FOUR

STUNNING STRANGER

With the last braid done, I stretched my arms out in front of me and leapt off my bed to join Dad downstairs. He had already prepared a generous plate for me.

As I took my first bite, the rich tomato-infused rice went down well with the tender spicy chicken. I didn't know if all Nigerian dishes tasted this good, but Dad's cooking was something else!

'Don't stress me out right now. I have a lot going on. I'll share the news when I can.' From his office, I could hear Dad arguing on the phone with someone.

What news? Was it to do with his job? Apart from the three-week trip, I wondered what else there was to tell.

He was now speaking in Yoruba, which I couldn't really understand since he never spoke it with me. I wanted to learn it, but when I tried to mimic his words, it never sounded right coming out of my mouth.

I made a mental note to ask what the conversation was all about. Right now, my focus was to enjoy my yummy dinner.

Moments later, Sinéad texted.

'Freedom has never tasted so sweet, see you tomorrow girl! xxxx.'

I had yet to tell her about how free we truly would be for the next three weeks. All I had told her was to come over tomorrow as I'd have the house to myself for the night. I wanted to see her face light up when I gave her the good news. So, I simply texted back: *'See you tomorrow'* along with a selfie of my new hair.

As I scrolled through my social media feeds, the posts of my classmates also enjoying their new-found freedom caught my eye. Some were sharing the beginning of their adventures, while others were complaining about how impossible the exams were and how glad they were to see the back of them.

While I caught up on the stream of updates, a notification popped up. Someone had liked a picture on my page; curious as ever, I tapped on the notification to see who it was.

All that was on my page was a picture of the sun setting outside my window, and Dad and me the day he decided to cut all his hair off. Three people had liked it – and now that number had increased to a total of four.

The new 'like' came from a woman called Folake, well at least that's what the account name suggested. A quick glance at her profile showed that she had an impressive 31k followers, this didn't seem to be a fake page or one of those accounts phishing for followers.

How did she find my page? Was it a mistake? Did she click on my profile accidentally?

The picture she had liked was an old one, so there was no way it had landed on her 'Explore Page', which I knew was one way people found new accounts. After all, both pictures on my page were from two years ago.

I scrolled through her pictures and posts; her profile was a bit of a puzzle. Her bio read, 'Find Me Where the Love Is' and beneath that she had both the Nigerian and Irish flag emojis.

The backgrounds of her recent pictures seemed familiar, and I realised I recognised some of the scenic locations around Clare and neighbouring counties.

My curiosity got the best of me, and I found myself clicking on more of her pictures. Nobody could argue with the fact that Folake was strikingly beautiful. I guessed that she could be in her mid-thirties, maybe even younger. She seemed confident and stylish. She was tall and slender with deep, chiselled features. Her afro was styled perfectly, framing her face, and highlighting her large, deer-like eyes.

Could she be a runway model? That would certainly make sense.

As I delved into Folake's world, I heard Dad's voice in the distance. 'Abi … Abi … ABI, what are you focused on?' he said, interrupting my deep investigation.

'Oh, nothing!' I replied, my trance broken, and without thinking I pressed the 'follow' button on Folake's page.

'Sorry about all the shouting, Abi!' Dad said, trying to sneak a peek at my phone. I quickly turned it face down, guarding my sudden fascination with Folake's profile.

'I didn't think work would call me on a Saturday, but you know how these people are!' Dad continued as he started to pile his empty plate high with food.

'Yeah, those unexpected work calls seem annoying,' I agreed. 'I heard something about telling me news. Then I couldn't understand the rest!'

Dad glanced up briefly from his plate before quickly returning his focus to his food. 'Oh, that? Don't worry about that, dear. It's just work stuff,' he replied, his tone slightly guarded.

His reaction suggested that there might be more to the story, but I decided not to press further. Dad's work problems were his own to deal with, and it seemed he wasn't ready to share the details.

As I stared at him eating, I couldn't help but wonder if there was more to his frequent travels than he let on.

Even if there was, I had my own thoughts to navigate, especially with Sinéad coming over tomorrow.

CHAPTER FIVE

A BIT HAIRY

Through the frosted glass of the front door, I could see a petite silhouette waiting patiently with what looked like a large school bag on their back. With a bottle of water in one hand, I jogged down the stairs to let Sinéad in.

'Hope I'm not too late, they were driving me up the wall at my place!' Sinéad said. Her schoolbag was weighing her down as though she had packed a month's worth of clothes for the sleepover.

I had asked her to arrive early, before Dad left for his flight – there was still an hour to go. I didn't want to give him a reason to change his mind about letting Sinéad stay while he was gone or even worse, change his mind about having Ms Kelly look after me.

Dad had spent the morning going over the responsibilities I'd have to keep on top of. 'Turn on the house alarm

44

before you sleep. Check that the windows are closed, make sure the stove is turned off.' There were many more instructions, but these were the ones that stuck out.

Sinéad pulled me in for a tight hug; she smelled like a detergent factory, a tell-tale sign that she'd been working with her mom that morning.

'Where is the man of the hour?' Sinéad asked, eyeing up the two large black suitcases in the hallway. She would use these formal phrases sometimes, things she'd picked up from her mother's customers, many of whom were keen to use banter as a way to earn a discount. I could hear her mom's voice in my head now, 'The price is the price,' she'd insist, with a face so stern it could put the fear right into you.

'I didn't want to tell you on the phone, but he'll be gone for three weeks … so you can sleep over for as long as you want,' I told Sinéad.

'Oh my!' Sinéad said, letting out a whoop of joy. She even started doing a little victory dance right there in the hallway. 'Oh, this is soo cool!'

I led her towards Dad's office, a little spare room at the end of the hallway. The room was small, but it just about fit his desk, chair and shelf full of paperwork. The door was slightly ajar and through the crack we could see him sitting at his desk, facing his computer with his head between his palms. He seemed to be deep in thought.

'Is he all right?' Sinéad whispered to me.

To be honest, I wasn't sure. He must have heard her though, because his head snapped up to reveal what I knew was a forced smile.

'Hello there, Sinéad! How are you?' Dad said, laying on his thick 'Irish' accent. I was always amazed by how seamlessly he could sound like he'd never set foot outside of Ireland.

'I'm good, Mr Benson,' replied Sinéad. 'Thanks for letting me sleep over a few nights while you're away! Oh, and Mam sends her greetings.'

Dad looked at both of us for a few seconds before he continued, 'Now, I know you girls are responsible, so I trust that you won't get into any trouble in the next three weeks … right?' His eyes were fixed on me, but the message was really for Sinéad.

Just as I'd suspected, Sinéad turned into an award-winning actor – even her body language changed while responding. 'It's so cool how you get to travel so much, Mr Benson! I didn't know you'd be gone for *that* long! I'm so happy … for you … I mean.'

Sinéad said this with the biggest smile on her face while nodding her head to prove how much she meant what she was saying. 'We'll be so good, on our absolute very, very *best* behaviour, Mr Benson, I promise you that.'

Dad wasn't fooled by her act in the slightest, but he also knew it was getting too late to consider a change of plan. His taxi would be outside soon.

Before leaving, he went over the house rules for the third time that day. He left me with some pocket money for the three weeks and instructed me to check in with Ms Kelly if I needed any help. I promised I would and when there were no instructions left to give, he wheeled his luggage into the back of the taxi that was waiting for him at the end of our road. We waved him goodbye and watched the car become a tiny dot in the distance.

Freedom at last!

We settled on the living room couch with a bowl of popcorn and some snake jellies. The plan was to marathon through some of our favourite reality shows, but I could feel Sinéad's eyes planted on me.

'I wish I could pull them off,' she sighed, picking up a single braid that was resting neatly on my lower back. With her fingertips she touched the top of my head and admired the lines that lay flat across my head.

'Don't mess it up!' I said, retreating quickly. 'It took me forever to put these braids in,' I explained.

'Sorry ... I just like this style a lot on you and ... and ...'

Something was holding her back from finishing her sentence.

'And?' I questioned, slightly irritated that she couldn't just appreciate my hair without touching, which she did a lot. Sinéad has always been a very touchy-feely type of person and since we're so close I understood why she felt touching my hair was no different, but I had warned her in the past that I didn't like it.

Sinéad hesitated for a moment before speaking. 'Is it OK for me to get braids, Abi?' she asked. 'Do you think it's like ... "offensive"?' She said this while doing air quotes around the word 'offensive'.

I had to let the question sit with me for a minute. I'd seen braids in many Celtic history books and films, so I knew it wasn't a style worn just by Black people, but Sinéad didn't want a thorough dissection of the differences in the reasons why people around the world wore braids. This was one of those situations where Sinéad was looking to me for guidance on something that she considered was part of Black culture, something she thought I'd understand.

In the past, I'd had to remind her that I was just about as clueless as she was. Apart from Dad, I didn't talk to any other Black people, and it's only been in recent years that I started to know more about Black history as well as Nigerian history. So even if I could answer her question, everything I had in my head was from the internet or Dad's perspective.

For me, topics on race left me feeling confused, and peeling back the layers of how I viewed myself made my stomach turn. So, I would just try to swallow down the inner conflict that often threatened to seep through my surface.

I've wanted to talk about my frustration with Sinéad, why her questions made me feel ashamed, but how would I reveal that I regularly threaded through the internet to understand why there were debates about Black culture?

In the past few months alone, there had been a lot of talk on social media about celebrities wearing hairstyles commonly seen on Black women. Some people were also telling stories about hair discrimination in schools and even at work. I couldn't help but put myself in their shoes. I'd feel so awful if a teacher at St Enda's sent me home for my current hairstyle.

The topic of Black hair was bigger than me and what I knew, so how could I be expected to take on such a large conversation? I decided to simply answer with what I had read in a recent article.

'I think it's important to be … mindful of the reasons you want braids and maybe even do some research on the style of the braid. Umm, but I don't think there's anything wrong with admitting you like a certain hairstyle worn by a Black person and knowing that it might not be right for you and your hair texture.'

I went on to explain everything I had learnt about the Fulani braids I did on myself and why she probably shouldn't wear it. Sinéad listened carefully to what I had to say and when I was finished, she confessed she'd always been curious about it all. I wanted to move on from the subject, but Sinéad wanted to talk more about hairstyles and was already scrolling through Instagram, highlighting some of the hairstyles that she thought she could pull off and that were more suited to her own hair texture.

Turning to me, she asked what I thought I could recreate. On her phone was an older woman who had similar jet-black hair to Sinéad. Bordering her face were two single braids sealed with a rubber band. The rest of her hair was in a ponytail with two fishtail braids on both sides. It looked really elegant.

I'd only ever tried to do my own hair, but if she was eager to change her look, I'd try my best.

'If you end up with a bird's nest for hair, don't blame me,' I half-joked, half-warned Sinéad. What else was I supposed to say? She wasn't one to take no for an answer.

I grabbed my bag of hair tools from my room and got to work. We passed the time playing hairdresser while the glow of the reality dating show on TV lit up the living room. Couples were being matched and muddled on the screen and we gave our own thoughts on the pairings at the end of each episode. In between, we plotted out our upcoming adventures for the next few days.

After what seemed like no time at all, I declared that I was done with Sinéad's hair. She wasted no time in grabbing her phone to use the front camera as a makeshift mirror.

'*Abi*, you're a genius! I look amazing,' she practically shouted, shaking her head to make her newly braided pony-tail sway. 'Have I always looked this good or is it the hair?' she teased while snapping pictures at different angles and uploading them to her Instagram.

'*Hair by Abi,*' she captioned the post, tagging me so I'd be able to share it with my followers too.

'I'm glad you like it,' I said, genuinely surprised by how happy it made her. I didn't think I'd done *that* good of a job.

As I looked at the pictures, I couldn't help but spot the flaws – uneven partings, inconsistent thickness on different braid strands. But if Sinéad felt confident and happy, maybe those imperfections didn't matter as much as I thought.

Our evening continued with a wardrobe raid. Sinéad was still stuck on trying to convince me to go to the upcoming disco in four days' time.

Deep down, I knew I had to find a way to divert her attention when disco day came around. I wasn't one to lie easily, but I had to come up with something convincing. A sudden sickness maybe? The wheels in my mind started turning as I mentally brainstormed a list of believable symptoms.

CHAPTER SIX

THRILLS AND FRILLS

Monday and Tuesday merged into one; we woke up, cooked store-bought pancakes, and spent the day switching between our phones and the latest sci-fi films.

Dad had sent exactly two voice notes, one to confirm that he had landed and was already knee deep in work, and a second one to let me know that if there were any emergencies, I could call, and he would answer instantly.

On this particular morning, though, we were getting slightly restless from being inside the house for so long, but the summer's heat and the idea of the long walk into town was a tiring thought. It was around midday when we decided that we couldn't do it anymore, we needed to leave the house.

We really didn't have a particular destination in mind, but it was important for Sinéad to avoid the route alongside her house, just in case her mam dragged us in for one of her infamous long chats or one of Sinéad's sisters forced her to cover their shift. They'd often promise to share their earnings and conveniently forget!

After a quick tidy up around the house, we made our way down the hill towards the shops. Sinéad had it in her head that should I change my mind, I'd need a dress that was 'DISCO' appropriate. She apparently already had one picked out for herself (by that she meant she had raided her sister's closet).

The sun was beating down on us and the refreshing cold bottle of water we were sharing between us started to taste like liquid gold. As we approached the main street, we saw the telltale signs of school being out.

The traffic that passed through the town was heading for the beach. It was easy to spot those who were local; we were dressed in fewer layers as the high temperatures felt like a rare but welcome treat.

There was a line of people outside a newsagent and a cluster of teens were walking out with cones of machine-whipped swirly vanilla ice cream. This must have caught both our eyes as we instinctively headed towards the line.

As we waited in the line, the sound of music and chatter filled the air. On days like these, I understood why American tourists would make Ennistymon a place of interest in their travels around Ireland.

We were now at the top of the line and the person operating the machine was a young girl who couldn't have been more than thirteen. She drew the ice cream, while an older boy, probably her brother, gathered the money into a grey tin box.

'Red or blue?' she asked with the two filled cones in one hand, nodding to the syrups on the table beside the machine.

'Both,' I replied, handing the boy the money, which he dropped straight into the tin which had a 'no change' label taped across it.

Delicious ice creams in hand, we slowly walked to the local boutique, 'Thrills and Frills'. It was where everyone went for any special occasion.

There was just a petite sales assistant behind the counter, and no other customers inside.

'You can't bring food in here,' she said sharply before we could even reach the clothes rack.

'This isn't food, it's a chewable dessert, and anyway we're basically finished,' Sinéad replied, then she cheekily shoved the rest of her ice-cream in her mouth, since it was just the crunchy end of her cone left.

I threw the rest of my cone into the bin by the shop entrance and avoided the assistant's glare.

She stared at us before continuing, 'Well, then, ... are you here for something in particular, ladies?' Her hands were folded in front of her as she scanned us like she was sizing us up. For what exactly, I couldn't tell.

We explained that we were looking for a summer dress, no flower prints, and certainly no puffy sleeves. The sales assistant smirked at us and directed us to the 'reductions' rack at the back of the shop.

I don't know if she thought she was being funny, but I was happy to scan through the rack of discounted dresses. After all, I didn't want to blow my pocket money on something I probably wouldn't wear anytime soon.

The only reason I agreed to the new-dress shopping spree was because I knew I could always keep it for my birthday next month!

Sinéad quickly got to work as though she was my personal stylist, showing me a range of dresses in different styles and colours. We both tried on dress after dress, twirling around in front of the mirrors and giggling at how some of them made us look!

'So will you be buying *any* of those dresses?' asked the sales assistant through gritted teeth; she had been pacing around the changing room each time we brought a dress in.

'We haven't found anything we like yet,' I replied, aware that she had been watching us the entire time we had been in the shop.

'What's your issue?' Sinéad snapped, her body language showing she was ready for an argument.

The sales assistant looked shocked and darted her eyes between the two of us. She then grabbed the two dresses out of Sinéad's hands. 'I know your family well! So, if you're not going to buy anything, begone with ya!'

The Sinéad's family had deep roots in Ennistymon, spanning generations. Sinéad's grandfather was a carpenter, and her grandmother was a seamstress. They managed to do well for themselves while raising their large family on very little money. In the late 1960s they decided to invest all their life's savings into the small launderette, so that their kids would have something to call their own.

Unfortunately, during this time their family's reputation took a hit when Sinéad's mother became pregnant with Margaret 'out of wedlock', as she would say.

The grandparents tried to hide her pregnancy by making her drop out of school, but it was too late as the gossip spread like wildfire.

As time went on, Ms Quinn met Sinéad's dad and they got married within three months of knowing each other. Their marriage lasted five years. During this time, Ms Quinn had Deirdre and Sinéad.

From what Sinéad has heard, her dad apparently took to the drink a little too much and would regularly come home unaware of his surroundings – the worst of it was when Ms Quinn found out he had also been secretly using a lot of the shop's earnings at the pub and had drained her savings.

When that marriage came to its end, Sinéad's mother found herself struggling alone with three young daughters to take care of. The launderette was never meant to double as a home, but she didn't have a choice. She ignored all the town's gossip about her illegitimate child and her failed marriage, and she worked tirelessly alongside her siblings to put food on the table.

The sales assistant looked at me and scowled. She opened her mouth to say something, but then pursed her lips together before turning on her heel.

Sinéad grabbed my hand, pulling me towards the door to leave. It didn't sit well with me that the shop assistant would get to go on about her day thinking the way she just treated us was right!

While I didn't particularly like anything in 'Thrills and Frills', a lilac silk dress caught my eye. I was drawn to its simplicity and, most importantly, it would prove the point I was trying to make.

I grabbed it and made my way to the till where the sales assistant was standing with the same bitter scowl painted across her face.

'I'd like to buy this,' I said plainly, placing the dress on the table. Beside the till was a rack of silver, pearl-drop earrings, which twinkled in the shop's light. 'And these too,' I added, looking directly in her eyes.

She didn't say anything, not that I needed her to. She scanned my items and bagged them. The price of the two pieces came to sixty-five euro, much more than I had anticipated spending. I counted the notes from my purse and handed them to her.

No pleasantries were exchanged during this interaction; you could cut the tension with a knife as she used one manicured finger to slide my change and receipt across the table.

Sinéad watched all of this from the shop door and when I turned to meet her, she had the biggest smile plastered across her face.

CHAPTER SEVEN

THE PERFECT PLAN

We were not going to let the incident at 'Thrills and Frills' cast a cloud over our day, so we decided to go to Vinny's for an early dinner.

Now that I had my new dress and earrings all bagged up, Sinéad wanted to 'get realistic' about our disco plans by figuring out how we'd even get there and back on our small budget.

All the money I had was for food or emergencies over the next three weeks and I had already spent some of it on the outfit I was carrying around.

Yes, I had savings I could have offered up, but I didn't want to give that as an option, and I knew Sinéad couldn't ask her sisters or cousins for fear that they would rat her out to her mom. If getting there was a problem we couldn't figure out, maybe she'd just let it go.

We were nearly at the entrance of Vinny's when I heard a faint voice call my name from the distance. I grabbed Sinéad's hands to stop her, while I looked around me to find the voice. 'Did you hear that?' I asked, turning to Sinéad.

'*Abi!*' screamed a female voice followed by the honking of a car's horn. At the same time, we both turned our heads towards a red Mini Cooper driving slowly towards us. There were three people in the car, but it was the driver that we spotted first as they had their window rolled all the way down.

'Abi, I've been trying to get a hold of you, haven't you checked your messages?' said the blonde girl who I immediately recognised once she took off the pair of white sunglasses that were hiding most of her face.

It was Clara Kelleher, one of the most 'crushed on' girls from St Enda's.

Clara and I have known each other since Montessori school. We were never close friends, but we'd been in classes together throughout the years. We were nice to each other and talked when paired for a class project, but outside of those fleeting interactions we could never find anything in common. As Clara's popularity grew, she became a little less approachable – or at least that's how other students viewed her.

So, to find out that she had been looking for me to the point where she thought to message me seemed incredibly strange!

Clara was wearing a yellow summer dress and had her hair tied up in a messy bun, though every strand of hair looked like it was perfectly curled and placed to highlight her stunning features.

'Abi doesn't really use her social media,' Sinéad replied on my behalf, noticing that I was having a very delayed response to what was happening.

I pulled my phone out of my bag to open the message Clara had sent me; it wasn't a text, which is why I missed it. Instead, she had sent the message two nights ago, through Instagram, in response to the recent post Sinéad had tagged me in.

Hey hun, love the hairstyle you did on Sinéad. It's very high fashion. Would you be able to do something similar for me on Disco night?

'Oh, I see the message now,' I said, raising my head, looking between Clara and Sinéad.

'So, what do you say?' Clara continued. 'Niamh and Shauna here usually help me with my hair for big events … but they're only good with a straightener or a curling wand!'

It was only then I realised who the other two figures in the car were – Clara's closest friends. Clara seemed to be the leader of their group and the other two girls always seemed to follow her around. They blindly did what she told them to do like she was their god. It had been this way since second year. I found myself wondering what brought them together. Looking at all three of them I wondered if it was their love of staying on top of fashion trends. Was that a strong enough foundation for friendship to be built on?

Niamh waved her hand from the passenger seat and Shauna gave us a half smile through the slightly tinted window of the back seat. I realised they were waiting for me to say something.

'Oh, I don't know …' I stated. I wasn't *that* good with hair. What I did for Sinéad was us just messing about and someone like Clara would expect perfection and I couldn't promise that, not even in the slightest.

'I'll pay you!' Clara said quickly, smiling sweetly at me like she thought that would work.

I wondered if Clara was always so quick to offer money when she wanted things. After all, she had a habit of hinting how well off her family was. She'd done this by showing off some of the luxury items she'd bought on shopping holidays with her mom or telling us about how important it was for her to keep up with high-fashion trends. She always had the latest of everything!

I thought of the last time I spoke to Clara; it was during a biology class we shared; the teacher had teamed us up for a project. Clara asked me what my college plans were and when I told her that I was hoping to study nursing at Trinity College, she genuinely seemed pleased.

At the time, I was expecting her to mention that she would be studying at some prestigious fashion university abroad, but instead, she quietly revealed that she too was hoping to attend Trinity. If all went to plan, she'd be there studying law from the comfort of an apartment her dad had been renting out.

'Us country girls will have to stick together,' she said with a wink, flashing that big white smile that made her so popular at school.

Sinéad was also staring at me now, waiting for my response to Clara's proposal. 'I was only messing around when I did her hair …' I started to explain, before Sinéad interjected.

'Abi's being modest, Clara, what she means is, she doesn't feel right taking money from you.' Sinéad was using her persuasive voice now, which meant she was up to something. 'Since we're all heading to the disco, though, what if Abi here does your hair … if we can both get a lift with you to the disco. I take it you're being dropped off, right?' asked Sinéad. Somehow, she made it sound like we were doing Clara a favour!

Clara thought about it, looked at Niamh and Shauna and looked back at us.

'Well …' Clara replied, letting the words roll out of her mouth slowly, 'I suppose that's not a bad idea! I'll let Mom know to be expecting two more.' She passed her phone to Niamh and muttered to her to text us her address.

'Abi, if you could make Sinéad's hair look that good, I can't wait to see what you can do with mine!' she said, clapping her hands together with excitement. I wondered if she knew how backhanded her comment sounded. Was it intentional?

'Come already dressed and no extra people!' Clara stated, grabbing the sunglasses that were perched on her head and once again covering half her face with them.

Niamh and Shauna didn't look too pleased with the plan and honestly, I couldn't blame them because neither was I!

Flashing one last famous smile at us, Clara rolled up her window and pulled out into the street, leaving us to return to the less glamorous reality of dinner at Vinny's.

CHAPTER EIGHT

WILD WORDS

'I can't believe Clara asked you to do her hair!' Sinéad exclaimed, grinning. Vinny's was now filled to the brim with people queuing. It was loud and busy, and the smell of fries filled the air, which made my stomach rumble loudly.

I don't know if it was because I was hungry, but I was very irritated. Even more so when Sinéad attempted to put a reassuring hand on my shoulder while we queued to order our meal.

'Don't worry, you'll do great. And if not, Clara can always wear a hat,' Sinéad said while chuckling at her own joke.

'What's *wrong* with you?'

The words burst out of me. I tried to rein it in so that the people around us wouldn't see the brewing anger that was probably plastered across my face.

'I *told* you I didn't want to go to this stupid disco night, and you keep pushing! Now, I'm going to have to pretend I know what I'm doing tomorrow, I'll probably end up knotting that girl's hair.'

The words were now pouring out of my mouth. 'It's just like in the shop today, you kept pushing us to try on those dresses and that woman thought we were going to steal them. Why can't you just *listen* to me for once?'

I was overwhelmed, I was tired, I was anxious. I couldn't find the words for all the emotions that were stirring in me.

'I think you're being unfair …' Sinéad replied, staring at me in confusion. 'You never said "I don't want to go", you said you "CAN'T" because of your dad and he's not around, is he?'

I was getting even madder now because she had a point, but I wasn't going to let her win this one; she *knew* I was reluctant and that should have been enough.

'I mean, we just bought the dress!' Sinéad continued. 'If you really don't want to do Clara's hair, you don't have to. I just thought it was the easiest way to get to Ennis without spending money. I saw the opportunity and I took it. And that lady in the shop was being a muppet, there was no predicting that!'

Sinéad was trying her best to calm me down and I was trying so hard to not sound like I was about to cry.

'But why do you want to go to this disco so badly? It's not even our scene.' I could feel my eyes water, and then I spotted Jack at the till, attending to customers. He would definitely ask why I was upset, and I didn't want that.

'Abi, we don't have to go if you don't want to,' Sinéad said. 'I guess the only reason I've been pushing so hard for this is because I know you'll have so many club nights to choose from when you go to college, I know it's stupid, but I just wanted to pretend I was sharing that with you.'

We were now near the top of the queue, only one customer between us and Jack. He was bagging her order for her as she counted her coins.

Deep down, I knew Sinéad had been struggling with the idea of change and not knowing what the future would look like for her. I knew there was a lot of change coming for me too, but I was pushing the reality of it all away. I figured I would face it all when September rolled around.

'What will it be for my girls?' said Jack while deepening his voice. I think it was an attempt to get a laugh out of us. The lady that was in front of us was now leaving with the bag full of food.

There was an uncomfortable silence between the three of us and it didn't take long for Jack to guess that something was off between Sinéad and me. His eyes were fixed on me, and I instantly felt a wave of heat run through my body. I avoided his gaze and stared at the menu behind him.

'You look upset, Abi, are you all right?' he asked. He seemed genuinely worried, but I didn't want him to get involved.

'Yeah, I'm good, just chips for me please,' I replied, trying to casually brush off his concern.

I was eager to move past this moment and leave Vinny's.

'Everything's good, Jack, we're just a bit hungry, bag of chips for me too please,' said Sinéad.

Reading between the lines, he didn't push for more answers, but kept his gaze fixed on me. 'I'll bring it to you,' he replied, and I simply nodded, determined to avoid direct eye contact.

Despite how busy Vinny's was, our favourite booth was free. Once we sat, I took a few deep breaths to calm myself before reaching out for Sinéad's hand. 'Let's go to your stupid disco and take a hat for Clara's hair, just in case!' I joked, trying to lighten the mood. I figured it wouldn't hurt to let her have this night even though it would stress me out. I mean, she was right: what were the chances of Dad, who was all the way in Nigeria, finding out that I went to a disco this one time? A little panic set into me as I agreed out loud, but I tried not to show it, especially since Jack was floating about.

The worry on Sinéad's face melted away as her lips curled in a half smile. 'I love you, you silly cow!' she joked back, leaning in to give me a loud audible kiss on the cheek.

'I see you've kissed and made up then?' Jack was now at our booth, holding up two bags of chips. 'These are on the house, just don't tell Vinny!' he said, winking at us.

Was this his attempt to cheer us up? If it was, I certainly wasn't going to complain about free chips!

'Aww, you shouldn't have, you're an absolute gent, Jack. It's a pity you're not my type!' said Sinéad teasingly.

Jack put a hand to his chest and tried to look like he was wincing in pain. 'Aghh, I'm so heartbroken. Rejected by the fair Sinéad Quinn.' His face was now scrunched up in fake agony.

He leaned in closer to our booth and directed his next words to me. 'And you, Abidemi Benson, am I not your type either?'

I felt caught off guard by the directness and weight of the question. Also, not many people from St Enda's called me Abidemi, not even the teachers, it was just 'Abi' to them even when reading the attendance list. I think many of the teachers gave up after first year because they struggled with how to pronounce 'Abidemi', but the fact that Jack said it so effortlessly, as though the name had been in his mouth before, seemed significant.

The air around us seemed to thicken.

'Umm …' was all I could say. I was really caught off guard by his question, his composure, and his ability to make me feel like I didn't have a single brain cell in my head.

He laughed aloud, a deep kind of laugh that caused some of the people sitting near us to turn their heads.

'Well, when you figure it out, let me know.' He paused, waiting to see if I had any follow-up statements. I just stared blankly, not even sure what kind of smart response would make sense. My palms were sweaty, and I felt my cheeks warm up.

A group of customers walked into Vinny's, adding to the growing line of frustrated people waiting to be answered by him at the till. 'See you around,' said Jack, smiling at us before turning to go back to work.

'*I think Jack likes you*,' Sinéad teased in a sing-song manner, sparks of joy in her eyes. I laughed at the thought of it because it could never be true.

Today was already filled with a lot of wild and unexpected events but to add to it, the idea that Jack Keane, one of the most crushed-on boys in Ennistymon, liked ME … was the most *ridiculous* part of it all!

I wasn't going to entertain the idea, not even for a second.

CHAPTER NINE

CAUGHT SOAP-HANDED

Before returning to my house that evening, we had to make a quick stop at Quinn's launderette. Sinéad wanted to grab her sister's dress, which she had washed in preparation for tomorrow night.

It wasn't a long walk from Vinny's to Sinéad's place; they were at opposite ends of the same street. It was well past opening hours at the launderette so there was no fear of being put to work by any of the Quinns.

'This is an in and out mission,' stated Sinéad. 'I don't want them asking me any questions about what we're up to.'

'Right!' I replied boldly. We both knew I was a terrible companion for 'missions' like these, my face gave everything away.

The shop was downstairs and Sinéad's family lived on the two floors above it. To avoid bumping into anyone, we chose not to use the back stairs like we normally would; that would have led us straight to the Quinns' kitchen. Instead, we used the front shop door, which Sinéad had her key to.

'Don't turn on the light!' she warned as we walked in. I brought out my phone so that we could use its flashlight to guide us.

Sinéad had hung the dress up on the clothes-collection rack behind the counter. Thinking ahead, she had covered it up and written a fake customer name on the tag.

'I guess I'm Miss Gannon tomorrow night,' she joked while folding up the black dress and putting it into a white paper bag.

As we turned to leave, smug about our successful mission, the shop light suddenly came on. Standing to the left of us, in front of the shelves where all the washing chemicals were kept, was a short silver-haired woman dressed in a long night robe.

'Now, WHAT in heaven are youse doing creeping around at THIS hour of the night?' said Ms Quinn, clearly unimpressed by our antics.

Sinéad and I froze, like deer in headlights, not knowing what to say.

Ms Quinn had a no-nonsense approach; it was how she kept both customers and her children from messing her about. She had perfected the stern look she now had on her face.

If we didn't produce a good cover story very quickly, we knew we would be in trouble. She of all people could not find out about our plans.

Sinéad leaned in to hug Ms Quinn, it was as if she was hoping the warm embrace would buy her some time to think.

'We didn't want to wake you, Mam,' she began. 'We were just trying to get some spare laundry powder in the back ...' Sinéad said, trying to keep a straight face.

Ms Quinn looked at us suspiciously, her eyes narrowing. 'At this time of the night? Why do you need it?'

Sinéad tried to think of an answer, but I could see her struggling. I stepped forward, my heart racing as I began to add to the lie that had been started. The last thing I wanted tonight was to get on Ms Quinn's bad side.

'Actually, it's a bit embarrassing ... I only realised today that I have no clean underwear left in my drawer. Since Dad's not around, there's a pile of dirty clothes that need to be looked after and I was planning on putting on a wash tonight.' I could not look away as she analysed my face, trying to decide if she believed me.

Ms Quinn raised an eyebrow. 'So, you came all this way for laundry powder when you could have just gone to the shops earlier?' she asked, looking at the bags we were holding in our hands.

'We forgot, Mam, it was so sunny, and we went around the shops. We hung out at Vinny's … we only just remembered now …' said Sinéad, trying to end all the questioning. 'Anyway, I got what we came for,' she added, pointing to the bag she was holding in her hand.

My palms were hot and sweaty now. What if Ms Quinn called Sinéad's bluff and asked to see what was inside the bag? Then we were really done for.

I looked down at my feet, trying to pretend I was too embarrassed to look at her; the reality was I was trying to hide how sweaty my face was.

'We're sorry to disturb you, Ms Quinn,' I said. 'I told Sinéad I didn't want to have to explain why we're here, that's why we came into the shop this late.'

As Ms Quinn took a few steps closer to us, we both held our breath waiting for her to ask us to reveal what was in the bag, but instead her eyes widened as she noticed Sinéad's hair.

'Did your day include a stop at the hairdressers then?' she said, walking closer to focus her eyes on Sinéad's head since she wasn't wearing her glasses. Sinéad grabbed at the chance to change the subject.

'Abi's got talent Mam, she did this for me,' Sinéad said, pointing at me. We both knew if we could keep her distracted, we would be in the clear.

'It wasn't too hard …' I added, still looking down.

'You'd do well with a gift like that, gal!' Ms Quinn said plainly; it was her way of complimenting.

She let out a sigh and then asked us to stay the night. When we said we'd rather go back to mine she started to insist we should stay, but then changed her mind when she heard children screaming from the floor above.

'*Christ,* will I have any rest in this house!' she shouted as though the voices creating all the noise could hear her. 'My brother's young ones are driving me up the wall,' she continued. 'I've put them in Sinéad's room for the night, so let me see if Deirdre is still around, she can give you a lift home.'

'That would be great, thank you, Ms Quinn,' I replied, genuinely grateful. I hadn't considered how dark it had gotten. I rarely ever stayed out this long and if I did, Dad was usually around to collect me.

With that, Ms Quinn called up to Deirdre, whose footsteps could be heard hammering down the wood of the stairs.

We made our way towards the back door. Parked in the alleyway was their family car, a slightly rusted grey Toyota that had certainly seen better days. Sinéad and I sat in the back and Deirdre, the middle child of the family, sat in the driver's seat.

She greeted us with a quick, 'Howya!' before starting the car engine that sometimes would cough fumes before it could move.

Deirdre and Sinéad fought a lot; maybe it was because although they looked alike they had completely opposite personalities. They were both tall with raven black hair, but unlike Sinéad, Deirdre's hair reached her waist and she always wore it down. I had never seen her without a full face of makeup. Her talon-like nails were always painted pink and even though it was late, tonight she smelled like she had just covered herself in strongly scented vanilla perfume.

For what was to be a ten-minute car ride, it didn't take long for Deirdre to start prying. 'So, I heard you were in the shops today?' she asked.

Sinéad and I shared a quick glance, unsure of how much to reveal. We chose not to respond, especially since it was her dress Sinéad had 'borrowed'. I pretended to be fixated on the road ahead, but Deirdre caught my eye in the wind-screen mirror.

'Are you seeing anyone then, Abi? I'd say you're nicer to the boys than our Sinéad is,' Deirdre remarked with a sly grin. 'I keep telling her to fix herself up.'

I didn't know if this was the big sister in Deirdre, but she would often try to get a rise out of Sinéad, any chance she got, and it would always work.

'Oh, piss off!' Sinéad said, pushing the back of the driver's seat.

This started a row between the Quinn sisters who bickered and shouted at each other, right up until we reached my front door. As soon as the car stopped, Sinéad stormed out of the car and I followed, thanking a very irritated Deirdre while I closed the door gently behind me.

'I don't know how you deal with her!' Deirdre complained, rolling her eyes before turning the car around to make her way down the hill.

Once inside the house, we did a quick check to make sure the windows and doors were locked. We then made our way upstairs, changed into our sleeping clothes and collapsed into bed.

We were exhausted from the day we just had, and I was nervous about the day we were about to have. Closing my eyes, I replayed the way Jack had said my name. I bit my lip to hide the smile my face was about to form. Even though the room was dark, I was scared Sinéad might just guess what I was thinking from my expression.

Her voice punched through my thoughts.

'Do you think we can pull this off?' whispered Sinéad, on the edge of sleep.

I pressed my face into her back. 'You've already figured out a way for us to get there, so yes!' I whispered back.

Strangely enough, I now felt a little excited about tomorrow, more than I'd admit. Maybe it was the idea of thumping loud music, having freedom to be a little bit reckless or the thought of letting loose on the dance floor. It all seemed so adult, so far from my normal.

I didn't know what to expect, but I was eager for all that tomorrow would bring. I was excited to get dressed up, to see the inside of Clara's house and finally understand why there was so much buzz around discos. Especially this one, the first of the summer. Would I love it so much that I'd become a regular? I tried to picture myself marching into the disco with authority and being welcomed like a celebrity. I had to hold in my laugh so Sinéad wouldn't wake up.

Tomorrow was a big day and as my mind started to slip away into dreamland, I took comfort in the fact that whatever happened, my best friend would be there by my side.

CHAPTER TEN

GLITTER AND GLAM

We spent most of the day anticipating when it would be the right time to start getting ready.

Before we made breakfast, we laid out our dresses and accessories on the bed. I chose to go for the pearl earrings I had just bought and a silver chain with a square diamond pendant.

A part of me considered wearing the only pair of black heels I owned, but after seeing Sinéad pull out her chunky boots, I decided comfort was more important. So, I went for a pair of white sandals with a large buckle on the side.

Finally, I was able to see Sinéad's black dress properly. It was double-laced with straps that formed into a sweetheart neckline. It looked enchanting and on Sinéad, who liked the Gothic look, I knew it would be fitting. She decided to pair her dress with a pair of white cross-shaped dangling earrings.

'Abi, I'm going to hop in the shower now so I can take my time with my makeup,' said Sinéad after what could have been our seventh episode of *Come Dine with Me*. Sinéad peeled herself off the sofa and I realised I hadn't thought about makeup.

It wasn't that I didn't wear it, I just didn't know how to make more of it. Lipstick and eyeliner were easy, but foundation, concealer and blush never seemed to work their magic on me like they did for the St Enda's glam girls.

Sinéad was lucky – she had two sisters who, often unwillingly, shared the same makeup, which meant she got good at it early on. The art of applying makeup became second nature to her. There'd been many mornings in our school bathroom where I'd stare at her as she applied it and I'd feel mesmerised.

The Quinn sisters also had the same complexion, which made it easier for Sinéad to raid their collection. Even Deirdre's darkest shade of 'caramel' foundation for when she was tanned worked as a bronzer for Sinéad, so she never had to think about buying the right shade.

When I first tried to get into makeup, I realised the shade range of foundations available in town left me with a greyish-green hue, so I had to research what foundation celebrities who looked like me were wearing.

I figured the singer Rihanna was the closest to my shade and I quickly went online to buy a range of makeup from her own brand. Finally, I was able to get the right honey-bronze tone that blended into my skin better. Applying it evenly was another hurdle; there was a lot of trial and error, some makeup-wipe casualties, but eventually, I felt confident in wearing a full face, even though I rarely had a reason to.

'Will you help me with my makeup when you're done?' I shouted to Sinéad who was already halfway up the stairs.

'Sure!' she shouted back.

Unable to take in any more of the show we were watching, I responded to a text from Dad who wanted to know how things were going.

I've been so busy, hope you're OK? Let me know if there are any problems.'

I texted back, *'All good here! xxx.'*

After a few more minutes of mindless scrolling on social media, my fingers found their way to this Folake lady's Instagram page. The most recent post was from twelve hours ago. A picture of her holding up a small brown dog. She was on a beach, so I zoomed in to the background surrounding her. Yes! I knew it, she was on Lahinch beach.

My hands hovered over the 'Like' button. I never really liked people's pictures online, I didn't want to give them reason to visit my very bland page, but this time, a part of me *wanted* Folake to visit my page again and for her to know that I could see her.

Without thinking too much about it, I posted the selfie I had sent to Sinéad a few days ago … this was the part I hated, trying to figure out what to caption a post.

'Happy Times', I typed slowly, spending a few seconds pondering whether to abandon the post and stick to my boring page.

Stop being a wimp, Abi, just do it! I said to myself.

I gulped in whatever air was left around me and pushed the 'post' button and instantly locked my phone.

Here's to trying new things, I thought to myself, *here's to being one of those carefree teenagers who don't overthink every little action.*

I could hear Sinéad's footsteps across the landing and with that I decided to make my way upstairs to get ready.

I don't think I have ever been so clean or smelled so good in all my life. I used a concoction of every body wash, perfume and facial product I owned. I'd seen what the girls from school looked like when they weren't in uniform and a part of me wanted to have just as much of a dramatic change in appearance. I didn't know if the extra scrubbing would do that, but it couldn't hurt to try!

Sinéad was already fully dressed, she looked great. I

couldn't believe that this dress was made for anyone but her. I watched as she paced from my bed, where her makeup was all laid out, to the standing mirror. Following the shape of her lips, she painted a deep red lipstick across her mouth while puckering and pouting so it would spread evenly.

'Perfect!' she said, pleased with her work.

'You look stunning!' I said, realising I had never seen her so dressed up.

'Thank you, m'dear,' she said, twirling in the little space that was left in my room.

I suddenly realised I was standing in my bath towel and wasn't sure how to get from what I currently looked like to anything near Sinéad's level of fabulousness.

A sinking feeling found its way from my stomach to my now wobbly feet.

'Umm ... should I put on my clothes first or will we do my face?' I asked Sinéad.

'First things first, sit down!' Sinéad said, grabbing a brush and pulling up my study chair in front of me. 'We need to find you a nice eyeshadow shade,' she said, looking at her makeup options beside me.

'Oh, I know ... a gold smoky eye,' she said, excited at the chance to get all artsy with a face other than her own.

With a pointed brush, she started to pat and dab shades of brown and gold across my eyes. Then came the eyeliner and mascara, which I knew I could do myself, but I let her have fun with it!

'OK, Abi, you need to do your foundation and I'll choose a lip colour combo for you!' she instructed. This might have been the most serious I had ever seen Sinéad.

As I plastered generous amounts of foundation and concealer all over my face, I could see my reflection transform in the small compact mirror Sinéad held in front of me. My eyes looked mysterious, and my skin appeared buttery smooth!

'Now, let's get to the finishing touches ...' Sinéad said, dropping the mirror and picking up a brown lipstick and what looked like pink blush.

I sat very still as she expertly patted colour into my cheeks and swiped an unexpected layer of sparkly gloss across my lips.

She got up and stood back to admire her work.

'A STAR IS BORN!' she belted out, her hands above her as though she was declaring this to an invisible audience.

I picked up the mirror to analyse the complete look. I *did* look good. I still looked like me, but older and more put together. I looked like the type of girl who had a perfect life and I liked how that felt.

'Now, get dressed and I'll wait at the bottom of the stairs like they do in those American films,' Sinéad instructed while sticking a tube of lip gloss and her phone into a small black handbag I realised was mine. I had never used it before, but it must have caught Sinéad's eye when she was raiding my wardrobe a few days back.

'Waiting at the stairs? Is this a teen romcom?' I asked jokingly.

'Only if you want it to be,' she teased, winking at me while practically prancing out of the room.

Once fully dressed, I stood in front of the full-length mirror. I had never worn a dress like this, one that hugged my often-hidden-away curves in all the right places. I breathed in, allowing myself to enjoy the moment. I liked this me! She looked cool and confident.

As I was admiring myself, Sinéad called out from the bottom of the stairs.

'Abi, are you ready? We need to leave soon.'

I grabbed a vaguely familiar round bag that Sinéad had left out for me. (How deep in my wardrobe had she gone?) I filled the bag with essentials: phone, keys, money and a small perfume bottle. I wasn't sure how sweaty a nightclub could be!

As I was packing, Sinéad shouted up again, 'Abi, where's the bag with all the hair products?' I froze. I had forgotten all about it, the reason we were going to Clara's and the disco in the first place.

I opened my bedside drawer and frantically searched for clips, combs and hair oil. I threw it all into the bag, which now could barely be closed.

'We look way too pretty to walk to Clara's house, Abi …' Sinéad declared as I joined her downstairs. 'So, I might have called a taxi while you were getting dressed. It shouldn't be more than a tenner, right?'

The front door was open and the taxi Sinéad had called was already outside. 'Are you ready for tonight, girl?' Sinéad asked, holding my hand while giving me a once-over. 'You look drop dead gorgeous, babe!'

This made me blush. 'Says you,' I replied, unsure of how to take the compliment.

I noticed one of Sinéad's braids was unravelling at the end. 'Remind me to fix this in the car!' I said, pointing to the rogue braid beside her earring.

'Don't worry about this,' Sinéad said, tucking the hair strands behind her ears. 'Focus those magic fingers on Clara's luscious locks.'

'Sure. No pressure!' I joked, knowing I was starting to feel all the pressure and anxiety once again in my stomach and legs.

CHAPTER ELEVEN

TANGLED UP

Clara's house wasn't far away, but it was in an area Sinéad and I had never been to. All we knew was that the further up that side of the hill you went, the bigger the houses were, and we were right.

We pulled up to a large two-storey white building with blossoming ivy creeping up the walls. In the front garden was a grey water fountain surrounded by colourful seasonal flowers and potted plants. As we walked up to the door, we passed what we knew was Clara's car, and two shiny white Jeeps!

'Have you ever seen the likes of it?' said Sinéad, rolling her eyes. 'Oh, how the other half live!'

Sinéad's comment made me pause and contemplate how she saw herself. I could understand her viewpoint – having grown up in a family where for the last ten years, everyone learned in and shared the one car, this display of abundance might have seemed to her like overkill.

The front door opened before we got to it and a blonde woman in a bright pink tracksuit stood waiting to greet us. No doubt, this was Clara's mom; they could easily be twins.

'Hi, girls!' she exclaimed in a very high-pitched tone. 'Come on in!' She gestured towards the hallway, making room for us to walk past her. 'Clara is upstairs getting ready with the others, she'll be down to you soon,' she said, ushering us in the direction of their front room.

Dotted around the room were professionally taken pictures of Clara at different ages. There was also a large, framed photograph over the fireplace; it felt strategically placed there because your eyes couldn't escape it. In the frame was the happy family standing together. The photo seemed like it was professionally shot in one of those white-walled photo studios. Looking as delicate as a flower was Clara dressed in a flowing red dress; she looked about thirteen years old. Clara's mom was dressed in a short, silky red dress that hugged her thin body tightly. In a black suit, with one arm wrapped around Clara's mom's waist, was a serious-looking bald man, Clara's dad.

To the right of the room was a large floor-to-ceiling glass cabinet; in it were certificates, medals and awards for various sports and achievements.

There was so much in the room, which I initially assumed was a living room. As there wasn't a TV but instead, pictures and wall art, I figured this must be the room guests were brought into.

There was, however, a large, inviting black leather sofa, which Clara's mom motioned for us to sit on. She flashed a beaming smile at us before leaving the room. As we waited in the silence, I couldn't stop looking around me. I was trying to take in more of the things that would give me a better glimpse into Clara's life. It was then I realised that what I once thought was Clara's boasting in school might not have been that; she was probably just sharing the extravagant reality of her world.

Sinéad, on the other hand, was uninterested and tired of waiting. She couldn't stop tapping her fingers on the arm of the sofa and she kept turning her head towards the door at the sound of footsteps walking past.

'What's with the waiting?' she said. 'I feel like I'm at the doctors!'

I didn't expect Sinéad to be as rattled as she was. She didn't seem to share an ounce of curiosity about our surroundings.

Funnily enough, Clara's mom did not to think it was rude to keep us waiting. Several slow minutes passed before she returned to offer us a bottle of cold water each.

'We couldn't go upstairs to them, could we?' Sinéad asked, trying her best to be polite and not sound annoyed.

Clara's mom smiled, the type of smile that didn't look like it connected with her eyes. 'They'll be down soon,' she replied, before once again leaving the room.

'If this were my mam and we had guests over there'd at least be a few nibbles put out,' Sinéad whispered, while sinking into the sofa in defeat.

More time passed before finally we heard excited voices and footsteps coming towards us. As the door swung open, Shauna, Niamh and Clara made their grand entrance, one after the other, their clackity heels announcing their arrival.

For the first time, I really saw Niamh and Shauna's individual style. Niamh was wearing a white, figure-hugging dress and Shauna was wearing a red skater dress. Both their dresses accentuated their long legs. They could be mistaken for the type of runway models you'd see on fashion programmes, especially in the way they confidently carried themselves.

However, it was Clara who truly stole the spotlight. She looked like a Hollywood actress straight off the red carpet. Her sparkly blue dress reminded me of a waterfall. The fabric draped and shimmered in the light. I wondered if she knew it was a disco she was going to. Surely this was the kind of dress you wore for a huge occasion like a boat party, an awards show ... or whatever events people like Clara went to!

It seemed that Clara was well aware she'd pulled out all the stops. She posed in front of us, allowing us to take it all in.

'You like?... Mom got it for me in Paris. It wasn't an easy find!' She shared this with a smug look on her face.

The only thing that was not yet perfect was Clara's hair. She had it up in a messy ponytail, waiting to be mastered.

Sinéad was the one to burst the bubble of awe I was in. 'Well, youse all look great, but time's ticking, do you want your hair done?' she said, in a hasty tone.

Clara did not like this. 'Sinéad, you look ... interesting! All black, though? You do know it's a summer disco not a funeral?' Clara said, making Shauna and Niamh snicker at the comment.

'Hmm ... charming as always!!' Sinéad said, not paying mind to the slight insult.

What Clara didn't understand was Sinéad had a large family and with that came a lot of sharp, witty tongues. I knew if Sinéad wanted to, she could tell Clara about herself, but she had a goal tonight, so she knew better than to unleash that side of her, at least for now.

I realised we had never all been in a room like this before and with the potential of growing tension, I spoke up.

'You do look very pretty, Clara. Do you still want the same style as Sinéad?' I asked, breaking the awkward silence between us all.

'Abi, you look so cute!' Clara said with a smile, pulling me in for an unexpected hug.

Cute? Something about being called 'cute' made me feel like a child, but I kept this thought to myself. It made me feel like I wasn't up to par with these girls. I thought about what Sinéad said a few days ago, about me turning eighteen and officially being a woman. Are women considered cute? The word lingered in my mind, creating a subtle discomfort. I tried to shake off the feeling and focused on Clara who was now reaching for the black band holding her hair up. She shook her head from side to side to let her hair loose.

'Actually, Abi, can you do the Kim Kardashian braids? I've seen it on you before. You know, the one that goes all back!' Clara gestured with her hands, tracing invisible patterns on her head to describe the hairstyle she wanted.

Her request caught me off guard, and a sinking feeling settled in my stomach. My body temperature rose as I struggled to find the right words to respond. 'Oh,' was all I managed to say, my voice betraying my discomfort.

Taking a moment to collect my thoughts, I cleared my throat 'Umm ... It shouldn't really be called "Kim Kardashian braids". It's just cornrows and I'm not sure if the style is right for you.' My voice trembled.

The room fell into an uneasy silence as my words hung

in the air. Clara furrowed her brows, a mix of confusion and surprise crossing her face. 'But why?' she asked.

I thought back to the conversation I had with Sinéad several days ago.

'That type of braid is traditionally done to protect hair types like mine ...' I began, my voice gradually steadying. 'But I can create a style that would be more suited to your hair type if you're OK with that.'

I made sure to give her an encouraging smile, so she didn't feel she had done anything wrong in asking. I'd never seen Clara angry, and I certainly didn't want her to be while we were in her home. Clara's expression seemed to waver, unsure of whether to respond or remain silent.

Niamh and Shauna returned with a chair from the kitchen, sensing the shift in the atmosphere since they left moments ago.

Clara's eyes met mine, and she finally spoke up. 'Sure thing, Abi ... I don't want to be considered ... insensitive.' She let the last word linger, its weight hanging in the air.

'That's not what I meant ... I just ... what I'm trying to say is...' I stumbled through strings of unfinished sentences.

Unexpectedly, Clara burst into laughter, leaving everyone in the room puzzled. 'Abi, relax, it's not that serious. Just make me look good.' The way she said this made it sound like a command rather than a request.

Clara motioned for Niamh to place the chair in front of me, and she sat down. I got up and emptied the contents of my bag. Grabbing my rat-tail comb, I began slowly and carefully parting Clara's hair down the middle.

'How do you feel about having two braids at the front and a braided bun?' I asked gently, admiring the softness of her hair, which carried a pleasant scent of strawberries.

'Go for it!' Clara replied, clapping her hands together.

Glancing to my left, I saw Sinéad offering a comforting smile and silently mouthing, 'Well done, Abi!' She then busied herself with her phone, pretending to be interested in whatever was on the screen. I figured she was trying to avoid engaging in conversation with the other girls.

As I quietly braided Clara's hair, her mother would occasionally come in to check on our progress. The three girls were focused on analysing the details of the latest local talk of cheating boyfriends and potential shop closures filled the room. At some point, I naturally tuned it all out and focused on the patterns I was creating on Clara's head.

Though I wasn't sure if Clara grasped the significance of what I had failed to fully explain, I was glad that I tried anyway. It would have felt uncomfortable to know that what Clara saw as a fashion statement held a deep historical meaning for Black women around the world. A historical meaning that I was still trying to fully understand myself.

CHAPTER TWELVE

PRETTY AND PROUD

The journey to the club felt like it was never going to end.

Clara's mom had booked a taxi driver, only the car didn't have any of the regular markings I was used to seeing.

'It's a private hire,' Clara explained, noticing my confusion at the presence of a strange, suited man in the driver's seat. I wasn't sure why we needed a 'private hire' just to go to the nightclub, but I nodded in approval so as not to seem ungrateful.

As we made our way towards Ennis town, Shauna kept asking the driver to turn up the radio when what she deemed her 'favourite song' came on. Then, as soon as the song ended, she would ask him to turn it down as she didn't want to listen to the 'boring' presenter on air.

For a moment, I felt bad for the driver, having to take

commands from screeching teenage girls, but after catching a glimpse of his unfazed expression, I figured he'd probably dealt with more annoying passengers.

Sinéad bobbed her head along to the Taylor Swift song, wearing a half smile on her face. She seemed amused by the chaos of it all.

It was strange to see Sinéad this way, especially in a group setting. If it had been her cousins or sisters, she'd be full of chat and sometimes exaggerated stories.

Finally, the taxi pulled into the street across from Electric nightclub, and the heavy bass music could be heard from its walls. A line of teenagers wrapped around the building, bunched up in small groups.

At the top of the line two tall security men stood – one bald, the other blond. The bald man opened and closed a rope fastened to the wall, while the blond man ushered people in.

Feeling overwhelmed, I looked over at Sinéad. She put her arm around my shoulders, pulling me in for a side hug.

'No backing out now, girl!' she said knowingly. I wasn't sure if she was trying to comfort me or herself.

'C'mon so Abi, let's go show off your work!' Clara said, twirling her freshly styled, braided hair around one finger. She had insisted on me finishing the style with half a can of hairspray, which nearly made me faint.

Her hair looked amazing, though, and I was proud of my work.

'Hold on a minute there, I'll get that for ye,' said the driver while unlocking his seat belt.

Niamh and Shauna were grinning ear to ear, adjusting their dresses, which kept revealing more than I wanted to see. The driver opened the door for us, letting in the dry, smoky air of the summer evening.

As we walked to the entrance, I could see a few familiar faces from St Enda's. I was sure some of the people in the line had already graduated a few years ago.

Many people in the line stared at our strange girl group. Their eyes followed us as we trailed behind Clara. She made sure to walk super slow, so the line could feast on her hair, her dress, but most importantly, her presence.

She walked past the line, and we followed, hesitant because we were skipping people who were there before us. Clara didn't even pay them any mind. She headed straight for the two bouncers at the top, while we silently waited a few steps behind her.

There was a lot of giggling between her and the bouncers.

'She always does this,' Shauna said, putting a hand on her hip.

'Well, it always works,' Niamh replied, linking her arm into Shauna's.

Whatever Clara had said to the two men clearly worked. The tall, blond bouncer stepped aside as Clara signalled at us to get in.

'Send my greetings to your mom!' the blond bouncer said to Clara, allowing her to enter ahead of everyone else before returning to his intimidating position at the front of the line.

Sinéad looked puzzled.

'Don't we have to pay twenty euro?' she said, revealing the wrinkly notes in her hands which she was ready to give as payment for entry.

This caused all three girls to burst into laughter and Sinéad's expression quickly turned to anger. Her face scrunched up as she prepared to speak her mind.

Before she could, Clara grabbed my hand and pulled me towards her, with Sinéad alone on one side and the four of us on the other.

'How's my hair looking? Is it still neat?' Clara asked.

I glanced at her hair and adjusted the two braids framing her face. 'You look fabulous, Clara,' I reassured her.

As we walked into the club from the courtyard, multicoloured laser lights flickered around the dark room. A few people were gathered in the centre, dancing to the DJ's remix of songs that were popular before I could even walk.

In the corners of the room, there were blue velvet sofas. On one end, a group of girls sat together, giggling, and pointing at a group of boys who pretended not to notice.

Another group of girls pulled out lipsticks and hairbrushes from their bags to touch up their hair and makeup.

I locked eyes with a short blonde girl I recognised from my after-school homework club. She discreetly poured something from her bag into the cup in front of her, pressed her finger to her lips, and winked at me.

Electric nightclub had a strict no-alcohol policy, but I guess some people found ways around it.

Clara and the girls quickly found their spot on the dance floor, right next to the DJ's booth. They twirled and bopped around, making sure everyone noticed their arrival, and soon a crowd began to gather around them.

'This is very different from what I imagined,' Sinéad commented, gesturing to the dance floor. 'I don't think I want to dance just yet.'

I breathed a sigh of relief. 'Me neither,' I replied, leaning closer to her ear as the music's bass grew louder. 'There's a small bar outside. Do you want something to drink?' The words felt mature coming out of my mouth. I accepted that tonight would be full of new experiences.

At the bar, a menu of mocktails displayed options like 'Pina-nolada', 'Gaga-rita' and 'Sorbet Sunrise', which seemed to be the most popular choices.

When it was my turn, Sinéad offered me the note that was still balled up in her hand from earlier. I took it, handed it to the barman and asked him for two 'Sorbet Sunrises'.'

'With or without ice?' he asked, unfolding the note to put into the till and handing back our change in coins.

'Without ice, these girls are cold enough!' a male voice chimed in from behind me.

Startled, I turned around to see who was brave enough to get an earful.

'Jack!' Sinéad exclaimed, leaning in to give him a hug. I was taken aback. I never considered that he would attend something like this, was this his type of scene?

'No hugs for me, Abi? I thought we were mates!' Jack said, grinning from ear to ear. We were holding up the line, so I stepped aside to let the next person order. I could only smile back at Jack because my mouth had gone dry; I felt caught off guard.

Jack looked different tonight. It wasn't just that I had only seen him in our school uniform or the greasy apron at Vinny's. I simply hadn't imagined him outside of those settings.

This evening, he wore black skinny jeans and a maroon button-up t-shirt. Beaded bracelets adorned his wrists, and a gold chain hung around his neck. His hair had more volume than usual, and his perfume smelt woody and fresh.

'Earth to Abi ... should I grab your drink for you?' Jack smiled, breaking my train of thought. I realised I had forgotten the drinks we had just ordered in my rush to leave the bar.

What's wrong with you, Abi? Get it together, I thought to myself.

'I'm good thanks, nice seeing you, Jack,' I replied while rushing to grab the two unclaimed ice-free red cups.

I wondered who Jack was with tonight. As I scanned the faces around him, I didn't spot any of the boys he hung out with at St Enda's, just some of our other classmates, but they were in their own groups already. Perhaps he was here with people who didn't go to St Enda's; there were after all some older looking boys near him. Or maybe he was here with a girl ... like a girlfriend.

The thought made me feel a bit uneasy. Before the situation could become any more awkward, I turned around and headed back towards the dance floor.

'Abi, wait up!' Sinéad called out, waving her goodbyes to Jack. She pulled me into a corner where several barrels doubled as makeshift tables. I handed her her drink.

'I think Jack really likes you,' Sinéad teased, making a love heart sign with her fingers. Taking a big gulp of her drink, she glanced over her shoulder back towards the bar.

'No, no, he doesn't ... I'm sure he already has a girlfriend or something!' I replied, trying not to have this conversation, especially here of all places. 'Also, it's just Jack, he just likes joking with us, that's all!'

Sinéad looked at me knowingly, her expression implying there was more to it. 'So, if you don't think Jack is into you, are you into him?' she questioned, cutting through my attempt to sidestep the topic. 'I tell you about who I'm crushing on or texting with, but you never want to talk about who catches your eye.'

It wasn't that I didn't want to talk about boys; I just never had many thoughts on the topic. Boys were just there, and I didn't think I was the type of girl that they were looking at in school. All the girls with boyfriends seemed confident and ready; they took pride in their relationships and seemed to effortlessly navigate the world of teenage romance. Even Sinéad, who knew she didn't want a boyfriend, had spent time with and even kissed the boys that she liked until they annoyed her.

As Sinéad's question hung in the air, I grappled with the realisation that maybe I hadn't given much consideration to boys because I believed they wouldn't give much consideration to me. The idea of being the centre of someone's romantic interest felt like a foreign concept.

Right behind Sinéad, I saw Clara, Shauna and Niamh emerging from the clubroom, fanning themselves with their hands. I tried to avoid eye contact – I didn't want them to walk in on this conversation or even guess what we were talking about. The last thing I needed was them giving me advice on my non-existent love life.

'*Abi*! There you are!' Clara exclaimed in her high-pitched voice. I pretended not to hear her.

'Ugh, here come the perfect trio,' Sinéad muttered. She didn't even need to turn around to know they were approaching us. She climbed onto the stool in front of her, preparing to stand her ground, and I did the same. Since there were only three stools, they wouldn't all be able to join us.

'I was looking all over for you, Abi,' Clara explained. I doubted it, but I smiled at her and gestured to our cups. 'We were just thirsty,' I replied.

Clara glanced at the drinks on our table. 'That's cute,' she said in a way that implied our drink choices weren't cute at all. I was starting to understand that 'cute' meant many different things to Clara.

'Come with us to the bar. I can get you something better. I'm good friends with Mikey,' Clara said, pointing to the bartender.

'Who aren't you friends with!' Sinéad muttered a little too loudly.

Clara smiled, her eyes fixed on me while her words were directed at Sinéad. 'Abi, can you ask your friend if she's OK?

I know she's dressed for a funeral, but she doesn't have to bring the mood down!' Clara said.

I felt like I was caught in the verbal crossfire between Sinéad and Clara. I felt like a referee in the ring, dodging loaded remarks left and right. I knew Clara was trying to get me to choose sides and that Sinéad had been a trooper all night, biting back her comments, but her patience was now wearing thin. It was like I was standing on a tightrope and they were holding both ends.

Meanwhile, I could now see Jack approaching us with a drink in his hand.

Could this moment get any worse?

'Hi, girls,' Jack said, unknowingly stepping in as a peace-keeper, positioning himself between Clara and Sinéad.

Clara's previously venomous look instantly softened, as if a lion had suddenly transformed into a delicate deer. She raised a hand to twirl a strand of her hair with her finger.

'Now, Jack, you didn't have to bring me a drink!' she giggled, attempting to flirt, I presumed. I couldn't help but wonder if they were compatible or if they had any history. Clara didn't strike me as Jack's usual type, but what even was his type?

'I actually didn't. This drink is mine,' Jack clarified, raising his left arm to show his own beverage. 'And this cup is filled with ice for Sinéad and Abi. I messed up their orders earlier,' he explained, placing the cup on our table with a bit too much force. A few ice cubes bounced out of the cup and onto Clara's heels.

Clara's gaze shifted from me to Jack, and then to Sinéad. She seemed to be trying to see the connection between the three of us.

'Tough crowd,' Jack said, breaking the tense staring competition between us and Clara.

With some frustration in her tone, Clara announced that she wanted to go ask the DJ something. Niamh and Shauna promptly joined her, forming their girl group with Clara leading the way as they walked back toward the clubroom, the sound of their heels clicking against the floor with more force than ever before.

'After that nonsense, I think I need to go to the bathroom,' Sinéad declared once the girls were out of sight. I was about to follow her, but she swiftly slipped off her stool. 'You two need to talk, so I'll make sure to take my time!' she said with a mischievous tone, quickly making her way out of sight before I could protest.

CHAPTER THIRTEEN

BUTTERFLIES BEGONE

This was the first time Jack and I had ever been alone.

Well, no, we weren't alone, we were surrounded by people, but still. We had never shared what now felt like such an intimate space together.

The mere presence of Jack had sparked something within me, turning my cheeks crimson and making my palms clammy. I took small sips from my cup, hoping to quell the butterflies in my stomach and avoid starting this conversation.

RELAX, Abi. It's just Jack … you've known him since primary school, I repeated to myself, trying to gather my thoughts.

I tried to pretend this was French class in St Enda's and he was sitting two rows behind me asking the teacher about tenses.

Nothing to be nervous about, Abi, just act normal.

Jack cleared his throat and broke the silence. 'Sorry about earlier!' he said, his voice carrying a mix of sincerity and nerves. 'I didn't mean what I said about you being cold. I was just trying to grab your attention.'

I mustered a response, trying to find my words. 'Oh, I wasn't offended or anything. I just didn't expect someone like you to be here,' I stammered.

'Someone like me, eh? Explain that now, Ms Benson,' Jack replied, a hint of amusement in his eyes.

My thoughts tangled and I looked away from his very, very handsome face. I was searching for something, anything, to distract myself. My heart raced, its rhythm matching the energy of the house music playing on the dancefloor. I struggled to find the right words, my mouth drying up. Any normal thoughts had fled from my mind.

In response to my awkwardness, Jack simply laughed.

Why was he so relaxed at a time like this?

'I heard you and Sinéad talk about coming here and I hoped I'd bump into you,' Jack explained. When I didn't respond, he continued. 'Remember, at Vinny's?'

I was taken aback and still had no words; it was like my brain had fogged up.

'Is it weird that I came? I just thought ... well ...' Jack continued, his voice trailing off. 'In my head, the plan was to accidentally bump into you, grab your attention, and ask you out on a date. I've wanted to for a while. But judging by your face ...'

As his words hung in the air, a surge of new emotions flooded through me. There was a part of me that was excited to hear him say what he just said, but there was also a part of me that was shocked to hear him confirm that he liked me. Enough to want to ask me out on a date. Like a real, proper date!

I had never allowed myself to think about Jack as more than just another student or the guy who served us our chips. If I did that, then I would have to be honest with myself. I would have to admit that maybe, just maybe, like some of the other girls, I too had a crush on him.

'A date?' I managed to utter, my voice accidentally revealing my excitement.

Taking this as a good sign, Jack reached for my hand. 'It's OK if you don't like me. I'll still serve you your chips,' he said, his words were playful as always.

This hand-holding was now making my heart start thumping against my ribcage. 'I've never been on a date,' I confessed, thinking about what Dad would think of this moment, 'but I think it would be nice... with you.'

A smile spread across Jack's face, lighting up his eyes. He leaned in closer, his warm breath tickling my cheek. The world around us seemed to fade away as he whispered, 'You look absolutely breathtaking, Abi.' The idea of taking some-one's breath with my exterior struck me as amusing – but I'd take 'breathtaking' over 'cute' any day.

Time stood still. The weight of unspoken words and hidden emotions was lifted off our shoulders. The noise from the party faded into the background and it felt as though it was just the two of us in our own little world.

Jack's face hovered so close to mine, and in that moment, I knew exactly what to do. I had never been kissed by a boy before, but I could sense Jack's uncertainty, he wasn't sure of his next move.

I closed the gap between us, turning my face slightly so his breath was on my lips. Jack's lips gently brushed against mine, sending a surge of electricity through my body. I melted at that moment. Now I understood what the hype was all about.

THIS FELT MAGICAL.

It could have been seconds or minutes or even an hour! Time no longer made sense.

I just knew that when Jack suddenly pulled away, I wished he hadn't stopped. Our eyes met and a shy smile lingered on both of our faces.

'Would you like to dance?' he asked, now holding both my hands in his.

'Um yes, but I think I should go find Sinéad first,' I replied, though deep down, I wished this moment could last forever.

Jack released one of my hands and reached into his back pocket, retrieving his phone.

'Put your number in here, and we can text. We have a first date to plan,' he said, a teasing tone in his voice.

CHAPTER FOURTEEN

THE EMPTY HOUSE

It was Sinéad's cousin Dean who rescued us from an uncomfortable car ride back with the 'perfect trio'. Sinéad had unexpectedly bumped into him on the way to the bathroom. They were both shocked to see each other in this setting. Unlike Sinéad, he was allowed to be there. She had to bribe him not to say anything to her mother. In return he wanted to be owed a future favour.

When I finally parted ways with Jack, who went to find the Callaghan brothers (who he'd come with), I spotted Sinéad with a group – her cousin, his girlfriend, and some other people I didn't know.

They went to Cillian's College, the secondary school here in Ennis town; they too had just finished their final year. What struck me about this friend group was they were easy-going; next to them, we looked overdressed. Jeans and

112

a nice top seemed to be their vibe, and to be honest, they looked way more comfortable than a lot of people here.

Dean's friends were genuinely interested in getting to know us. They asked questions about how our exams went and what we got up to during the week.

Sinéad's mood had drastically changed for what felt like the third time that evening; she was being a bit distant and on high alert. I took charge of answering Dean's friends' questions and told them all about how glad we were to see the back of St Enda's, the terrible experience at 'Thrills and Frills' and how strange it had been to be in Clara's house all evening.

The last part seemed to catch their attention. 'They live in that big house with the fountain out front, don't they?' one of Dean's friends asked, surprise evident in his tone.

'You can't miss it, that's for sure,' Sinéad finally chimed in.

'Hmm … my mam does her round of cleaning there at the weekend. She loves it because they tip really well!' said Dean's friend.

'You know you've made it when you can have someone round to clean up after you. One day, lads, one day!' Dean said.

Thoughts of Anne who came to clean our house on the weekend came to mind. Did that make me more privileged than I thought? The contrast between our perspectives left a pang of guilt in my chest, especially when I caught Sinéad's glance at me, but thankfully another one of Dean's friends changed the topic.

'Sinéad, did you hear that our Dean here is thinking of doing night classes for a business certificate? He'll actually have to use his brain for once!' This made the group laugh, and even Sinéad chuckled. I didn't understand what seemed to be an inside joke, but I laughed too while also looking beyond the group to see if I could spot Jack in the distance amongst the growing crowd.

We spent an easy hour bantering with the group until Dean announced that he was heading home early as tomorrow was his first day at his summer job as a lifeguard in the local swimming pool.

We overheard Dean whisper to his girlfriend to say her goodbyes so he could drop her home. Sinéad interrupted to beg Dean to give us a lift too.

I wondered if Clara would be relieved or mad that we didn't come to find her. I didn't know if the offer to drop us was even still on the table, so I said nothing and let Sinéad secure our way home.

'It won't take you that long,' Dean's girlfriend said, siding with Sinéad as Dean reluctantly agreed.

I quickly texted Clara: 'heading home, got a lift, thanks for today'. I silently prayed that she didn't take it personally that we dashed off so suddenly after all the earlier tension.

On the other hand, I was excited to have this time to tell Sinéad all about what happened when she left for the bathroom. I made a mental note to drop hints in the car but to actually wait till it was just us to give her a full breakdown.

'The launderette, yeah?' Dean asked once we reached the car park.

Sinéad glanced at me nervously. 'Could you drop Abi first?' she asked. 'She's just up by Church Hill.'

This surprised me. Naturally, I had assumed we would return to my place together, as we had been doing all week. Didn't she want to hear about what happened with Jack? After all, she encouraged it.

I was trying to catch her eye as we got into Dean's car. She just looked ahead and kept chatting to Dean and his girlfriend who were sitting in the front. Was she purposely avoiding eye contact? During the car ride, all I wanted to do was to talk to Sinéad, but she was now too busy talking about how disappointing the disco was, it seemed it didn't live up to her expectations.

'Everything OK?' I whispered to her, once there was a lull in conversation.

'Of course, babe!' she responded, smiling at me.

I replayed the events of the night in my mind, searching for any clues I might have missed. Sinéad had seemed fine before she left Jack and me. I knew Clara had annoyed her all night, but I didn't think it would make her be weird with me.

'Did Clara annoy you again? Did she turn up in the bathroom?' I asked, slightly worried.

'Clara's lucky she didn't catch me in the bathroom,' Sinéad said in a hushed tone before continuing, 'I got talking to some girls from my Art class, they've got great plans for after the summer, they're all so excited.' With that last part she seemed distant, and I didn't know what follow-up question to ask so I left it.

When we arrived at my place, Sinéad simply said, 'Text when you're in bed.'

'You didn't ask me about how things went with Jack,' I said, feeling dismissed and slightly hurt.

'I'm just tired, Abi, but I do want to know everything. Text me, OK?' she replied, reaching over me to open the door.

Dean waited until I entered the house before vanishing into the night. As I settled into bed, I realised all the excitement I had about my kiss with Jack had become overshadowed since Sinéad had been cold towards me during that car ride.

Did I say something? Was there something I did or didn't do? Was she mad that I was trying to keep things sweet with Clara and her friends?

Once I was ready for bed and tucked into the comfort of

my sheets, I realised the house felt different with nobody in it. I was missing Dad for the first time since he'd left.

I reached for my phone to see if he had texted. He hadn't, but I had an Instagram notification. It was Folake, the lady whose profile page I found myself revisiting. She had finally followed me back, and I found myself surprisingly pleased by this small interaction.

I clicked on her profile picture, which had a glowing red ring around it; this meant she had posted something in the last twenty-four hours.

Staring back at me was a picture of Folake in a bright pink crop top and high-waisted leggings. She had on black sunglasses and her afro was in two little puffs.

In her arms she was holding a small brown dog. They were posing in what looked like a park.

Folake seemed so cool, cooler than anybody I knew, and I desperately wanted to know more about her.

Since we now followed each other, I could message her – the option wasn't there before on her profile.

I don't know where the courage came from, but my fingers grazed over the 'message' button under her picture, and I began typing before I could think too deeply about how weird it was to reach out to an online stranger. So many out of the ordinary things had already happened tonight, what was one more thing to add to that list?

'Hi, you seem cool. I'd love to meet you and I can even do your hair… if you ever need someone to!'

I imagined she was a celebrity and I was a fan. Would she open the message, laugh at it then close it again? Or worse, would she see the message notification and ignore it, adding it to the list of weirdos who don't understand that being social media friends means nothing in real life?

Deep down, reaching out to Folake felt like more than just a casual interaction. Maybe, just maybe, there was a part of me that was looking for a Black female role model, someone who exuded the confidence and coolness I wanted for myself. Maybe, in reaching out, I was hoping for a connection that could fill that gap. I felt incredibly lame, adding to the mountain of emotions I was already enveloped by.

Accepting that at this stage. I had nothing to lose, I pressed the send icon. I turned my phone off and pushed it under my pillow. If I stared at my words, I would start to overthink them.

I closed my eyes and tried to breathe out all the tension I had been holding in after all of tonight's big moments. The only thing that would not leave my mind was the memory of Jack's face so close to mine. I let myself imagine that maybe he too was now in his bed, replaying our first kiss! It was a nice thought to fall asleep to.

CHAPTER FIFTEEN

DAYDREAMING

I woke up abruptly to the sound of loud banging on the front door. With a yawn, I untangled myself from the comfort of my bed and cautiously made my way to the front door.

The silhouettes of two figures came into focus as the sleep started to clear from my eyes.

'Abi, are you OK?' The familiar elderly voice pierced through.

Oh no! It was Ms Kelly. I had completely forgotten that Dad had told her to check in on me!

I swung the door open to be met with the concerned faces of Ms Kelly and Anne, our cleaner. Anne's arms were tightly folded against her chest, and she looked visibly annoyed.

'Abi, are you OK?' Ms Kelly asked again, scanning me as I stood at the door in my oversized shirt.

I cleared my throat, my voice still raspy from sudden use. 'Yes, I'm fine,' I replied, trying to compose myself.

Anne chimed in angrily, 'I pressed the bell for ten minutes! Why didn't you answer?'

'I'm sorry ... I was sleeping and didn't hear the bell,' I replied.

'I'm running behind by half an hour,' Anne said. 'So, are you going to let me in?'

Feeling flustered, I opened the door wider to allow both Anne and Ms Kelly to enter. Anne brushed past me, clicking her teeth in disapproval, and headed straight for the kitchen.

Ms Kelly placed a comforting hand on my shoulder. 'She was just worried when you didn't answer. She knows your dad's away, so she came to ask me if I had a spare key to check up on you.'

'Oh!' I replied, staring blankly at the short grey-haired woman that stood before me.

Ms Kelly continued, 'I was worried too. I should have stopped by sooner, but I've been so busy getting things ready for the church bake sale tomorrow.' Ms Kelly then went on to complain about the chaos of organising people.

Conscious of my morning breath, I interrupted her mid-sentence to ask if I could go brush my teeth.

Ms Kelly looked at me, as if realising for the first time that I wasn't properly dressed. 'Of course, dear! Don't mind me talking your ear off,' she said, chuckling. 'Oh, and look!' She held up a small basket filled with brown eggs. 'A gift from my chickens, I figured you might need them more than I do.'

I gratefully accepted the basket, thanking her for the thoughtfulness. I couldn't bring myself to tell her that my dad had already stocked the fridge with two dozen eggs before he left.

'Well, I hope you're not too lost with your dad away. I know you're grown now, but if you ever get bored or need a meal from an old lady, do come over!' Ms Kelly said warmly, giving me a tight hug.

After Anne had left, and I had taken the time to wash and feed myself, I realised that I still hadn't heard from Sinéad, which was unusual. Folake hadn't replied to my message from last night, and Jack hadn't sent a text either.

As the day went on, I realised that Sinéad's presence had helped me ignore the anxious state I'm usually in when alone with my thoughts for too long.

I wanted to make the most of my day and push aside the lingering frustrations I was feeling. I allowed my imagination to wander and pretended I had just moved into a large penthouse apartment in Dublin city and just like they do in those 'country girl who moves to the big city' film scenes, I connected my playlist to the living room speaker and swayed to the beat that filled the empty room.

This is what living alone is like, Abi. You decide how you want to feel and what you want to do.

I vaguely recognised the song that came on next because it had played when we entered Electric nightclub. My imagined penthouse transformed to the dancefloor of the club.

I was now dancing with Jack, and we were surrounded by familiar faces who were cheering us on.

I could see Clara, Niamh and Shauna staring and pointing and Sinéad was clapping in support. Some of the boys from St Enda's started to form a line, revealing square pieces of paper with letters on them that had appeared from thin air.

'WILL YOU BE MY GIRLFRIEND?' the letters read. Jack held my hand and looked into my eyes, patiently awaiting my response.

The crowd was now shouting. 'Say yes! Say yes! Say yes!'

'Aghhh!' I screamed, my toe had bumped into something hard and the clang of it falling jolted me out of my daydream. The iron tool by the fireplace had fallen and remnants of ash and coal now stained my feet and the once glistening hardwood floor; Anne would be *soo* pissed!

With a slightly bruised toe and a mess around me, I decided that enough was enough. I was going to call Sinéad and tell her off.

My phone vibrated in my hand as soon as I picked it up and Folake's profile image popped up. Excitement surged through me while I slowly read her message.

'Hi, Abi! It's nice to hear from you, thanks for the offer, hope you have a good day.'

A smile spread across my face as I read her response. A part of me wasn't sure that she'd reply, but she had. She actually opened my message and typed words back. An idea crept into my head and in my excitement, I typed it straight into my phone.

'Are you free tomorrow by any chance?'

I stared at my phone for what felt like ten minutes as the 'typing…' icon kept popping up and disappearing. Did I overstep? Was she trying to find a nice long way to say 'no'?

'I'll be bringing my dog to the vet tomorrow' Folake replied.

Hmm. Did that mean she wasn't free, or did she not understand my message? I couldn't imagine a vet appointment taking the whole day, unless the dog was really sick. I decided to be direct about why I was asking about her availability in case she didn't really understand the text.

'Hope your dog is OK! I was asking if you're free because I'd love to meet you in person. I completely understand if you don't want to or think it's a bit strange, I just think you're cool and would love to get to know you since based on your pictures, it seems you live nearby, I promise I'm not weird.'

There. That's as direct as I could be. If she said no, I'd understand, she probably had a very busy life, but at least I tried.

The 'typing' icon appeared again. And then ...

You're a very sweet girl, Abi, and no, I don't think it's strange, I just don't know if meeting is a good idea,' she replied.

My heart sank. I didn't want to come across as pushy, but I wanted to show that I understood where she was coming from and that my intentions were genuine. After all, if the roles were reversed and someone online asked me to meet up in person, I'd also be as hesitant.

'I get it. Safety first, right? How about this – I can send you a pic of my student card or whatever you need to prove I'm just an ordinary, not-so-weird person?' I texted back.

'I have no doubt you're who you say you are, Abi. No need for the ID check! Let's do it this way, I'll be at Ryan's Café around noon, we can share a quick coffee?'

A mix of excitement and nervousness surged through me, and I quickly agreed. *'Awesome! Looking forward to it. Noon at Ryan's it is!'*

Folake simply replied with a *'See you then'*, but that was enough for me.

The frustrations from earlier melted away as I thought about all the questions I wanted to ask Folake in our now locked-in meet-up. Where was she from? Why did she move here? What did she do for work? Did she have family here?

I felt so infatuated with the idea of getting to know her. Folake represented something I hadn't had much of in my area. Something I didn't know I longed for, an unspoken connection that often comes from shared experiences. I wanted to know what growing up around Black people was like for her and how different it now felt living somewhere where there wasn't a Black community. I felt like I could learn a lot from her.

Now with plans to look forward to, any frustrations I had from earlier were nowhere to be found. I decided that I'd stop by Sinéad's tomorrow to tell her all about Folake and maybe even convince her to come to Vinny's with me. I also wondered what interacting with Jack would feel like now that we'd shared a kiss.

I decided to spend the rest of my evening in the kitchen as I was craving Dad's cooking. One of my favourite dishes he often makes is Nigerian fried rice. What made the fried rice 'Nigerian' was the use of habanero chilli pepper, Nigerian seasoning cubes and homemade chicken broth. The aroma in the air made me feel like Dad was there with me.

I wondered how he would react if he knew I was meeting a mysterious woman from Instagram. The idea of his face contorted with worry made me laugh a little.

BRAIDS TAKE A DAY

As the evening settled in, I decided to have my dinner out in the garden so I could savour the warm summer breeze. Sunset shades of pink and orange filled the sky, darkening slowly as I munched away.

CHAPTER SIXTEEN

GROWN WOMAN

My plan was to pick a nice seat and wait for Folake. I figured it would make me appear less nervous than I was. I had on a little makeup and even some red lipstick, which wasn't something I'd normally wear, but I wanted to look a little older.

When I arrived at Ryan's Cafe, Folake was already there. She was sitting by the window tying her dog's leash to the handle of her chair. I slowed down my steps as I got closer, my heart racing as I took in her full presence. She was even prettier in person. There she was before me wearing a long dark green dress, looking effortlessly elegant.

When she raised her head, she could see me staring. 'Abi, right?' she asked, reaching her arm out.

'Yes, that's me,' I replied. 'Nice to finally meet you,' I said, shaking her hand.

I awkwardly planted myself in the seat across from her, all the talking points I had rehearsed in my head were nowhere to be found.

I was focused on her hair, her afro puffed out like a cloud around her face. Folake broke my trance and asked me what I wanted from the menu on the table between us.

I scanned the list of sandwiches and cakes, remembering that I hadn't had any breakfast that morning, but I was also too on edge to eat. Maybe I'd just go for something to drink.

'Maybe a vanilla latte?' Folake said, filling the long silence. I nodded in agreement. I figured that the vanilla might mask the taste of coffee, which I wasn't a big fan of.

'Cool, I'll have that too,' Folake said, getting up to go order at the counter. 'Make sure Oba doesn't run off,' she said, pointing to the brown dog that was now sniffing at the crumbs of whatever leftover treat was beneath my chair.

Folake returned to the table with a slice of chocolate cake and two spoons. My stomach rumbled at the sight.

'I couldn't resist ordering this,' she said with a smile. 'The coffee will be here soon.' As she dug into the cake, she motioned for me to do the same. I took this moment to launch into my first question.

'So, what brought you to Ennistymon?' I asked before shoving a large spoonful into my mouth while the tension in my shoulders started to disappear.

Folake leaned back in her chair, looking thoughtful. 'I moved from Nigeria earlier this year,' she began. 'I wanted change, and the opportunity came so I said why not!'

'Opportunity?' I asked, puzzled. 'Like work?'

'Something like that...' she said while smiling at the server who was now hovering beside us with two cups.

Folake took a long sip of her coffee before continuing. 'Back home, I was an interior designer and I loved it, but I've recently had to change my focus and now do what I do, but online.'

'What does that mean?' I asked.

Folake smiled. She found this question amusing. 'Basically, it means I can help people plan what the inside of their home will look like without having to meet them in person.'

'Do you like what you do?' I asked.

'Yes, I do! Since I moved here, though, I'm learning that Irish people have less colourful taste than I'm used to. In Nigerian homes, MORE is MORE! It's been a bit hard getting clients here, but I'm trying ...' she said.

Folake's accent was unlike any Nigerian accent I had heard before. At times, it sounded British, other times, it sounded American.

'Enough about me, tell me about you.'

'Oh, me? I've never worked, I just finished school!' I replied.

Folake laughed. 'I know that. What I meant was what would you like to be? Or what would you like to study!'

'Oh, I think I want to be a nurse, at least that's what I hope to get the points for,' I responded.

'You *think*?' Folake said, her eyes scanning me. 'You don't sound excited.'

'Well, my dad suggested it and I'm pretty good at science, so I figured why not!' I said.

'Hmmm ...' Folake didn't look like she agreed with my answer. 'And the hair stuff? Is that a hobby?'

'I like doing hair, but I haven't done anyone's hair apart from my own, my friend Sinéad's and this girl called Clara,' I replied. I wondered if I should tell her about the reasons I even started doing my own hair. How the bad haircuts, the painfully tightly braided roots, and the heat-damaged curls I suffered at the hands of many hairdressers over the years pushed me to finding my own solution. I knew she'd understand, but I didn't want to dampen the conversation, so I decided to explain it in a different way.

'After some bad experiences, I started to watch a lot of videos online about different hairstyles that I'd either like to try on myself or practise on other people. I hope it doesn't sound weird, but I find everything to do with hair very relaxing, seeing the creativity that goes into transforming someone, taking the time to plan out the style, being aware of how different haircuts, colours, shapes and textures can change a person's face. It's so purposeful and thoughtful. Then one day, I found these videos of Black women who talk about the history of different braided hairstyles while they install the style on themselves, and I just thought it was the coolest thing ever. I became obsessed with learning more and doing the braids on myself, just like these.' I pointed to my head. 'They're called Fulani braids.'

Folake stared at me smiling, while taking in every word. I suddenly felt too seen and this made me very conscious.

'That's why I offered to do your hair ... to practise on someone other than myself. That is, if you want me to, I mean your hair already looks so nice!'

'From the sounds of it, doing hair is not just a hobby, it's something you can imagine yourself doing professionally?' Folake asked.

'I've never thought about it as a job.' My heart thumped in my chest as I considered Folake's question. I wondered what Dad would think. He'd probably disapprove. Dad would disapprove of *a lot* of the things I'd been doing in his absence.

'It's always been just a way for me to express myself and take care of my hair since it's so curly and thick. I don't know how realistic it would be to pursue it as an actual job.'

'You know,' Folake said, 'sometimes the things we're passionate about can turn into incredible careers. It's worth exploring since it's something that brings you joy. I'm sure there are plenty of people who also struggle to find someone who knows how to work with hair types like ours or even just someone who clearly wants to make sure that people have good hair care and leave feeling beautifully transformed.'

Hair like ours! The way Folake said it made it feel like we were friends, like we had something in common. She fully understood where I was coming from and didn't make me feel weird for caring about hair so much. This made me feel closer to her and less self-conscious.

I wondered if this was what it felt like to have an older sister, an auntie or even an older cousin. The idea of a shared bond, especially in something as personal as Black hair, created a sense of connection and warmth that went beyond the surface of a casual friendship. Would this have been what it was like if I had lived in Nigeria surrounded by extended family?

The thought lingered in my mind, and a touch of longing for a familial connection I hadn't experienced grew stronger. This need went far beyond anything Dad could ever provide. Was this because he didn't see life the way a Black woman would?

I thought back to the experience I had when looking for makeup in my shade. I never talked to Dad about it, I never mentioned it to Sinéad or Ms Kelly, but if, just maybe if, I had grown up with someone like Folake, or if Mom was alive, it wouldn't have been such a lonely experience.

Between sips of coffee, we chatted more, and as crazy as it sounds, I knew I needed this person I had just met to be in my life. She wasn't just cool; she was smart and open. She shared a lot about herself, and as I learned more about Folake's life in Nigeria, I imagined myself as her in the stories she told.

She was born into a big family. In a line-up of six siblings she came as the fourth child. Most of her twenties she spent travelling. She had always been independent and adventurous, so her choosing to move to Ireland didn't come as a surprise to her family and friends.

Surprising myself, I too told her about my own boring life, what it was like growing up in Ennistymon, how we lost Mom to cancer, Dad's new job and how it changed things for him. I even told her about Sinéad's antics, Clara's bossiness and a bit about the teenage disco … without the whole kissing Jack part. I felt that was a bit much.

I wasn't expecting how easy it would be to talk to Folake. The conversation only stopped when Oba started to bark when another dog twice his size came in.

'Guess it's time to bring this one home!' Folake said, picking him up and placing him on her lap.

'Oba has had a busy day … he was so well behaved at the vets for his annual check-up, he's getting old now, but thankfully he's still healthy!' she said, holding him close so she could kiss him. Oba's tail wagged happily in agreement.

Sensing that she was getting ready to leave, I blurted out, 'I really enjoyed meeting you! Can we do this again?'

I knew if she had stayed the whole afternoon at the café, I would have too. Folake made me feel heard in a way I didn't realise I needed.

'Umm …' Folake said, 'I'll tell you what, why don't you tell your dad about us meeting first. I'd feel more comfortable. And then you can come to mine to practise your hair skills on this bush,' she said, pointing to her hair.

'I'm sure it won't be a problem,' I said, even though deep down I knew I wasn't going to ask Dad. I wanted to keep Folake all to myself for a bit. I felt a surge of excitement at the idea of meeting up with her again, seeing the inside of her house, getting to know more about her life and even the prospect of styling her beautiful afro.

Folake got up and held both her arms out, 'Come let me give you a hug before I go.' I stood up and awkwardly fell into her warm hug, her buttery-sweet perfume smell tickling my nose.

When Folake left Ryan's Cafe with Oba trotting happily by her side, I felt a rare stirring inside me, a need to know her more. I never had someone I could be in awe of, but today, that certainly changed.

CHAPTER SEVENTEEN

BITTER TASTE

What was I going to say to Sinéad when I met up with her? Would she approve of me meeting with this online-stranger-turned-friend? How would I even begin to describe Folake?

I decided I'd only tell Sinéad about my day if she asked me. After all, I really wanted to know what she had been up to all this time. It just wasn't like her to not have been in touch for two whole days.

The last time Sinéad was this distant, it was when her dad had unexpectedly started writing letters to her from a Dublin address. He was sending the same letter to her and her sisters. At first, it seemed as though he was trying to reconnect with them, so they wrote back. It didn't take long for them to realise that the only reason he was writing to them was because he needed money. Deirdre and Margaret stopped writing to him, but Sinéad didn't. The sisters fought for weeks about this until Sinéad stopped.

I considered that maybe it was something to do with him. Family stuff can be complicated, heavy even. So, I'd completely understand, but maybe she didn't think I would.

As these thoughts filled my head on my walk towards Sinéad's place, I noticed that the sun was now shrinking behind a growing grey cloud. Rain would come soon, and I didn't have a hoodie or an umbrella with me.

Even though I was unsure of what mood Sinéad would be in once I got to hers, I was still hoping that once we talked, she would ask me to stay the night.

Maybe we could even get a round of chips for ourselves and her family to share. I smiled, remembering the days where I would join the Quinns at their dinner table and listen to their latest life lessons.

Two little girls were crossing the street, giggling while poking each other with the dull, white plastic forks in their hands. A woman was running after them with a large brown paper bag, which had splotches of grease. They must have just come out of Vinny's.

I slowed down my steps to see if I could make out the shape of who was serving today. Vinny's door was wide open, but a scattered queue of people waiting around the counter meant I couldn't see much without inching closer. I didn't want to be creepy by standing there, trying to catch a glimpse through squinted eyes, so I let it go and kept walking up the road.

I was sure that once I told Sinéad that Jack hadn't called me, she herself would march down to Vinny's to give him an earful.

Trickles of rain began to wet the ground in small circular patterns and by the time I got to the end of the road, the church bell started to ring to signal six o'clock.

I was surprised to spot Sinéad standing at the frame of the shop door, shielding her body from the rain. In front of her was a figure. They had the hood of their jumper up, so I couldn't make out their face. From their frame though, I was fairly sure it was a boy.

I stopped beside a large green postbox so I could hide myself better. I could only really see his back, but the way the boy moved seemed familiar. I was too far away to hear what they were laughing about, and it wasn't until the boy threw his head back in laughter, causing his hood to fall down, that I recognised his face.

My teeth clenched and my ears turned hot.

Why was Jack with Sinéad?

I crouched down behind the postbox, shrinking myself as small as possible. I was now practically kneeling on the wet ground. The two people I had been waiting to hear back from were together and seemed to be having a great time too.

Jack wasn't a customer of the Quinns. If he was, he would have had a bag full of laundry with him, but there he was laughing with empty hands.

They had always cracked jokes while we were in Vinny's or in St Enda's, but for Jack to make his way out here? What on earth did they have in common?

All the potential reasoning running through my head was crushed when they hugged!

The coffee and cake I had earlier turned in my stomach and I felt a bitter taste in my mouth. I had to hold on to the postbox as my eyes welled up. I had to remind myself to unclench my teeth and breathe.

Did they have something going on? Was this why they had both been avoiding me?

I thought about whether I had missed signs of Sinéad also liking Jack. If she did, why hadn't she said anything and why would she encourage me to talk to him? And if Jack liked Sinéad, then why kiss me? He came across as honest and sincere. Maybe this was just a game for him? Maybe I was just a chase?

That nauseous churning feeling came over me again. I watched as Sinéad and Jack waved goodbye to each other. I watched as Jack jogged in the direction of Vinny's. I watched as Sinéad entered the launderette, flipping the door sign to 'Closed.'

It was as though the universe was playing a cruel trick on me, drenching me in rain as I grappled with the storm of emotions inside me. My wet clothes clung uncomfortably to my body, reminding me that I couldn't stay here all evening.

Pick yourself up, Abi! You can do this.

I took a deep breath and stepped out from behind the postbox where I had been hiding. My steps felt heavy, like they were carrying the weight of the world with them as I trudged towards home in the rain.

I didn't get far though.

I heard a car horn blaring behind me. I turned around and saw a white Jeep pulling up beside me. 'Hey, what are you doing out in the rain?' yelled a high-pitched voice.

My vision was blurry, so I quickly wiped the tears and the rain from my eyes. It was Clara and her mom in the Jeep, looking at me with worried expressions.

I tried to put on a smile, even though it was obvious I had been crying. 'Just trying to get home,' I managed to say, my voice catching slightly.

'Well, then, hop in, you'll catch a cold in this,' Clara's mom said, giving me no room to argue. I climbed into the back seat.

CHAPTER EIGHTEEN

CHAMOMILE TEA

'**A**re you OK, Abi?' Clara asked gently from the passenger seat, her voice full of empathy.

I sighed, finally letting my tears betray me. I was no longer able to hold back the flood of emotions. I tried to wipe my face with my wet sleeve, but only ended up staining it with the mascara and red lipstick I forgot I was wearing. I must have looked frightening.

'I saw something today,' I said through sniffles, my voice barely a whisper.

Clara fully turned her body, I had her full attention now. She pushed her head in the gap between her and her mom's seat. 'What did you see?' she said sharply, unable to hide her curiosity.

I hesitated, not sure if I was ready to put my thoughts into words, how it would even sound. I didn't know if Clara was the safest person to trust with what I was about to reveal, but the weight of it felt suffocating, like there was pressure in my chest. All I knew was that I needed to ease the pressure. I needed someone to talk to, someone who might help me make sense of it all.

'I saw Sinéad with Jack,' I finally confessed, my voice trembling. 'They were together, laughing, hugging ... It felt like ... I don't know, like I'd walked in on something.'

Clara's eyes widened, and she exchanged a quick glance with her mom, who was very much tuned in to our conversation. Her body leaned back in her seat as though she didn't want to miss a word I had to say.

'I just don't understand,' I continued, my voice shaking. 'Why would she encourage *me* to talk to Jack if ... if there was something between them?'

'I didn't know you were talking to Jack!' Clara said, looking puzzled. 'Like in a "more than friends" way?'

'Well, we weren't ... then we were ... then we kissed!' I said.

Clara's eyes widened further in surprise. 'Wait, you and Jack *kissed*?' She sounded like it was the most unimaginable thing ever. 'I didn't think you were his type or he yours,' she said. If I wasn't so upset, I'd be slightly offended.

I nodded, feeling a mix of embarrassment and frustration at my own situation. I didn't want Clara's mom to see me in a different light, to think that I was a bad influence and all I cared about was boys and kissing. 'Yeah, it was a surprise to me too. He told me he liked me, and I guess I like … liked him too.'

Clara's expression shifted from surprise to concern, and she glanced at her mom again, exchanging another silent message of understanding.

'Abi, boys say a lot of things that they don't mean,' Clara said softly, trying to establish her maturity in these matters.

Tears welled up in my eyes again, but this time it was different. 'I just don't know what to think anymore,' I admitted, my voice wavering.

This time, it was Clara's mom that replied.

'Abi, you seem sweet, so you might not know this yet, but relationships can be messy and complicated, and people's actions don't always make sense,' she said.

I wiped my eyes with the back of my hand, smudging my makeup even more.

Clara chimed in, 'If I had a penny for every boy at St Enda's that's flirted with me, then tried to flirt with Shauna and Niamh, I'd be a millionaire! Boys are silly like that,' she said, in what I assumed was an attempt to comfort me, but also stroke her own ego. A part of me wanted to ask if Jack had ever flirted with her, but I knew this wasn't the time for that. I found solace in the fact that Clara, with her casual remark, was attempting to offer some form of support.

It wasn't until my tears dried up that I realised we weren't heading towards my house.

'I'm up the hill, Mrs Kelleher,' I said, aware of my surroundings again. I was worried that she might not know where I lived.

'Clara mentioned that your dad's not around at the moment, so you can stay with us for the night! You're in no shape to be home alone crying over a boy,' she said.

While I would have preferred to go home and have a good cry underneath my duvet, I was grateful for the offer. Being minded didn't sound so bad.

'Thanks, Mrs Kelleher,' I said.

I felt both fascinated and jealous of the closeness that Clara and her mom had, and I found myself longing for mine. I wondered what advice she would have given me about boys and heartbreak. How would she have comforted me? Would I feel comfortable enough to tell her all this?

As we pulled up to their house, I couldn't help but find it funny that I was seeking refuge in the home Sinéad felt so uncomfortable in. Especially in my most vulnerable state.

Once inside, Mrs Kelleher showed me where the guest bathroom was and handed me a fluffy towel and an oversized sleeping shirt. 'You can run yourself a bath, the water is still warm,' she said emptying out a drawer full of bath products.

Closing the door behind me, I placed the towel on a nearby hook and started to fill the bathtub with warm water. I squeezed a plastic bottle of lavender-scented soap in, which started to foam up.

I carefully slipped into the bath, sinking my whole body underneath. I closed my eyes to drown out the looping image of Sinéad hugging Jack and when my mind attempted to think of them kissing, I balled my fist up to push the thought out.

'How are you feeling now?' Clara asked when I entered the kitchen, following the sound of clanging cups and a boiling kettle.

She and her mom were sitting across from each other. Both had changed into pink pyjamas. This and white seemed to be the dominant colours in their house.

For the first time in a long time, I saw Clara's face without any makeup. I had forgotten that as a kid she had freckles spread across her cheeks. They were even more visible now and made her look her age.

'I feel better,' I said, standing there awkwardly as Clara gave me a sympathetic smile and pointed a steaming cup in my direction, saying, 'It's chamomile tea with honey.'

I took the tea and let it warm my hands. I wasn't sure what to do with myself, but I didn't want to sit down in case they asked me more questions about what I had shared in the car.

Mrs Kelleher just stared at me intensely. It was almost as though she was waiting for me to fall apart again.

'The bath helped, thanks.' I wanted to establish that I was really OK now. 'I'm really tired,' I said, faking a deep yawn.

'Of course you are! Clara, be a dear and show her the guest room,' Mrs Kelleher said.

Clara rolled her eyes, slightly annoyed at her mom's hosting skills. 'She can sleep in my room. She's my friend, Mom.'

Were we really friends now? Could we confide in each other about our lives? I suppose I'd already done that, so there was no going back. If Clara now considered me her friend and felt comfortable to have me in her room, it made sense to be open to the idea of being friends with her. I wondered how a certain someone would feel about that.

Clara led me to her room where the walls were adorned with fashion posters and fairy lights. She took a seat on her bed.

'I've had my fair share of confusing moments when it comes to boys and sneaky friends, but we'll be off to college soon and all of this won't matter so much!' she said matter-of-factly.

I sighed, unsure of whether I would now categorise Sinéad as a sneaky friend. I still didn't want to think what I saw was what I saw. But if it *was*, then where would I put

Sinéad in my head? 'I just wish things were simpler, you know?' I replied.

Clara shifted to make room for me on the bed. 'I get it, believe me, but you'll be OK, this will all blow over.'

CHAPTER NINETEEN

MOM'S LOVE

'Down in the dumps' couldn't even describe the way I was feeling; I was just trying my best to be OK with what I had discovered.

When I got home from Clara's, I went over to Ms Kelly's house, and I helped her make some cookies, label her homemade jam, and get eggs from her chickens. It felt nice to keep my hands busy and to spend a day talking about simpler things.

I wasn't my usual cheerful self and Ms Kelly assumed it was because I was missing Dad. She kept reassuring me that he'd be back soon. She even offered to bring me to mass with her that evening. I smiled and made an excuse about having stuff to do at home. I didn't feel like faking a smile with people.

Sinéad had called me a couple of times and Jack texted asking when I was free to meet up. I didn't answer, I put both on mute. Whatever deceptive game they were playing, I didn't want to be a part of it.

Dad would be back in a little over a week and I figured maybe it would be better if I just stayed alone for the rest of the summer. Two months of solitude before college couldn't be that bad.

Clara was being super nice, she kept texting me to ask if I was OK and if there were any updates. She even added me to her group chat with Shauna and Niamh where they shared memes, fashion hacks, celebrity news and commented on what they thought of people's social media posts. I'd text back a 'thumbs up' emoji now and then, but I wasn't all that interested in what they had to say. I just didn't want to come across as ungrateful by removing myself from the chat.

Annoyingly, Clara had told them in the group chat that Sinéad got with Jack even though she knew I liked him. The way she wrote it in text made it sound so scandalous; while I didn't tell her it was a secret, I was irritated that she had shared what I told her in private. Niamh and Shauna were shocked and said some not very nice things to which I just didn't respond, even if they were trying to make me feel better.

Today, though, I found myself missing Mom more than usual. I imagined my head on her lap while she gently stroked my hair, assuring me that everything would be OK in her soft, soothing voice.

In an attempt to feel closer to her, I decided to visit the spare room. It was a space we rarely entered; it held memories of Mom's last days at home before she had to stay in the hospital in Limerick.

During that period, Mom's immune system was incredibly weak. The doctors had warned us that she had to keep away from any unclean areas that might hold a lot of bacteria that could impact her health. It was a challenging time.

That's when Anne, the cleaner, came into the picture. Mom's mom took the initiative to arrange for Anne to clean the house regularly as it was a lot for Dad to take on alone while also looking after me.

The light bulb in the spare room no longer worked so I opened the curtains to let some sunlight in. It felt colder than the rest of the house. Some years ago, Dad had packed away most of Mom's belongings as well as things that reminded him too much of her. They were taped up in boxes placed around the room. Most of it was clothes that he just couldn't bring himself to donate to our local charity shops, even though Anne had offered to do it for him plenty of times.

I carefully went through some of the boxes, cleaning dust off the many items. One of the boxes held pictures, some in albums, some in frames and some bundled together with a rubber band.

Many of the pictures showed my parents in their younger days. In one picture, they were both holding pint glasses up, in another, Mom was wearing a ballgown and Dad was wearing an oversized suit. Most of the pictures were of them posing in front of different landscapes and buildings.

There was one picture that caught my eye – it showed Mom wrapped up in a hospital robe, a radiant smile on her face. Her hair looked messy, and her face was slightly flushed. She was holding up a little yellow blanket, and inside it was a baby version of me, my eyes still closed. I had seen this same yellow blanket in one of the other boxes, now a bit faded and creased up.

Another picture I spotted was still in a frame. It was of me, a little older, my dress covered in green paint. Mom was beside me, her cheek pressed against mine, wearing a blouse that was also covered in paint. I was maybe about four years old in the picture. We were both holding brushes with more paint on us than on the pages laid out on the kitchen table. I thought seeing these pictures would make me sad, but instead, I felt a mix of joy and longing.

I decided to take this picture out of its frame. I wanted to hold on to it and bring it with me to college. As I undid the clasp of the frame, I noticed faint writing on the back. I brought it closer to the window to read the words that had been penned there.

'*My dear Abi. Hold onto dreams, let kindness be your guide. You're a piece of my heart, a part of my soul. In your journey ahead, may you stay whole.*'

It felt incredible to see words written by her, left for me. It was as if her voice was reaching out to comfort and guide me, even in her absence.

I took a picture of the writing and sent it to Dad, who didn't take long to respond with a call.

'Hey, Abi,' his voice greeted me warmly through the phone.

'Hey, Dad,' I replied, realising I was also missing hearing his voice. 'What did you think of what Mom wrote? I found it in the spare room.'

There was a pause on the other end. 'It's amazing,' he said. 'Your mom was amazing with words, much better than me.'

I smiled as though he could see me through the phone, 'It's like she's still looking out for me, even now.'

'That's because she is, she always will be,' Dad said gently. 'How've you been? Sorry I haven't been in touch that much.'

I hesitated for a moment. It wasn't like I could tell Dad what was really going on and I didn't want to lie either. Choosing to divert from the topic, I simply replied, 'Let's just say I can't wait for you to get back.'

Dad chuckled at this. 'Already tired of taking care of the house then! I can't wait to be back too. It's been too long, how about we plan something special for the weekend once I'm home? I have so much to tell you.'

A smile tugged at the corners of my lips, I felt a sense of relief at his words. 'That sounds perfect, Dad. I'll be counting down the days.'

'Me too, Abi,' he said warmly.

It felt comforting to connect with him again, yet our conversation also made me realise how much had changed in such a short time. I didn't even feel like the daughter he had said goodbye to. We continued to chat, discussing his busy schedule and my own outings. I filtered out many details though, especially about recent events.

After saying our goodbyes and hanging up, I found myself staring at the message Mom had left me once more. I read the words repeatedly, absorbing their meaning until they were etched into my memory.

'May you stay whole!' This line felt like what I needed to hear; it struck a chord within me. Despite the challenges I was currently facing, these words reminded me that my mom's love would always be with me.

CHAPTER TWENTY

LAYERS OF TRUTH

'Is this comfortable enough?' I thought to myself, holding up two nearly identical leggings that I had just taken out of the dryer. I chose the one that looked less worn.

I analysed my choice in the mirror, shrugging my shoulders. I felt I looked somewhat put together. My combination of a beige tartan shirt, black leggings, and red converse was cute, but, more importantly, I felt comfortable.

While I was making breakfast, I texted Folake to ask if she was free. When she didn't reply I texted again to let her know I was free.

'Hi Abi, nice to hear from you again. I'm working from home today,' Folake replied.

I texted back, 'I'm free to do your hair, if you still want, I told my dad about our meeting, he said it's fine.'

OK, that last part was a *big* little lie, I hadn't told Dad anything, but how would she know that and how would he find out?

With all the boy drama I had been trying to get over, I had pushed my meeting with Folake to the back of my mind, but this morning she was the first person I thought of. I was once again brought back to our fun chats and laughter at Ryan's Café. Since I already felt like Folake was someone I could talk to honestly, she would have good advice for me, and I really wanted to see her again. About an hour passed before she finally texted back. I was starting to get scared that she might leave my message on 'seen' and ignore it.

'I do need my hair done for a meeting tomorrow, how about I collect you? Please make <u>sure to tell your dad.</u>'

Why was she being so persistent about me letting Dad know? Was she that concerned about safety? I chose to ignore the last part of her message as we planned for later that afternoon.

Comb … edge control … hair grips … setting spray, I threw all the hair essentials into my yellow tote bag.

Folake sent a pin to her location, and I sent her mine. I had always assumed that Folake lived in Ennistymon, yet it turned out that her house was situated in Lahinch, a charming beach town just a five-minute drive from here. If I could drive, I would meet up with her every day.

From my window I could see a blue Nissan Micra making its way up the hill. Even from this distance, her distinct silhouette was unmistakable. I hurried downstairs to meet her at the door, flinging my heavy yellow tote bag over my shoulder.

'Hey, Abi!' Folake greeted me with so much enthusiasm like we were friends who hadn't seen each other in a long time. Oba barked from the back seat, revealing his face and pressing his paws against the window as if he was greeting me too.

'Hi!' I responded, a huge smile plastered across my face.

'Your home is so beautiful; you can see so much from here,' she said, taking her time to visually explore the house and its hillside surroundings while I locked the front door.

'Yeah, this is us, been here my whole life,' I replied, trying to see the house through her eyes. I was suddenly conscious about how overgrown the grass had gotten and the slightly weathered paint.

Folake's face seemed to approve though. 'It's a lovely place, Abi, it seems peaceful.'

Oba excitedly barked in agreement and Folake chuckled. 'And it seems Oba likes it too.'

'It's not so bad at all,' I replied, taking pride in our area.

The drive was short and calming, the warmth of the sun bathing everything around us. As the car turned a corner, a small blue bungalow came into view at the end of a row of similarly shaped homes, all facing the seafront.

I hadn't known what to expect of Folake's home, but what I saw inside was surprising. A burst of colours and mismatched artwork adorned every corner. The walls were painted in citrus yellow, and shiny black door handles gleamed against them.

A series of loosely painted brown lines depicted a stylised female face across three canvases, drawing me in with their shape. Beige wooden floors contrasted with feathered dark lighting fixtures hanging from the ceiling in the hallway.

Entering the kitchen was like stepping into a playful dream. Bright blue cabinets and red appliances stood in vibrant contrast to the marble white counter tops, and yet somehow, they all tastefully complemented one another. There was no traditional dining table. Just an open and airy space at the back of the kitchen.

Natural light streamed in through double glass doors, which Folake opened to let Oba out into the small, enclosed garden.

'Wow. I don't think I've ever been in a house quite like this,' I remarked, genuinely impressed by the unique decor.

Folake laughed, her eyes gleaming with satisfaction. 'I told you I'm an interior designer gone rogue. When I moved to Ireland, I wanted our home to be fun. I won't be in this house forever, so I just went a bit mad with it.'

'Our home?' I asked, suddenly realising that she might have a boyfriend she lived with or maybe a husband, I never even thought to ask. She was wearing multiple rings, so it was hard to tell if the one occupying the fourth finger on her left hand meant anything.

She must not have heard me though, so I didn't ask again.

'I didn't know a home could be this ...' I continued struggling to find a single word to describe the wildness of Folake's home. She was either a genius or completely off her rocker.

Folake gestured toward her garden where there was a picnic bench that I sat on. I watched as Oba played between the potted plants and the two trees a hammock was hanging from.

'I have some fresh juice, tea and coffee, what would you like?' Folake asked.

'Fresh juice sounds great,' I replied.

Folake emerged from her vibrant kitchen with a jug of orange juice and two empty glasses. She placed them on the bench and took a seat across from me.

'Perhaps you can do my hair outside? It's such a lovely afternoon, and I want to tan,' she teased, her laughter con-tagious as she enjoyed her own joke.

'Sure, let's make the most of this sunshine,' I said, realising I could practically smell the beach air from here.

Once I had finished my juice, I carefully began emptying the contents of my bag onto the table.

'Any particular hairstyle you have in mind?' I asked, my fingers shaking. I was a bit scared to mess up her gorgeous afro hair.

'Just make me look like a Nigerian queen,' she said, a playful glint in her eyes. 'I want to pepper my haters,' she added in a song-like voice that brought out her Nigerian accent even more.

I couldn't help but laugh too. She was already regal looking; a hairstyle couldn't change that.

With a gentle touch, I began combing and stretching out her hair, relying on my instincts to guide me through the process. I planned out the intricate pattern, then applied some edge control around the perimeters of her head.

Her hair was completely different from mine. She also opted for no extensions – she wanted to keep it natural. As I weaved and twisted, I made sure each braid was tight and precise.

'So, Abi …' Folake began, her voice curious, 'I'm guessing you didn't actually ask your dad for permission to come over?'

My hands hesitated in Folake's hair, and I could feel a blush creeping up my cheeks. How did she know?

'I, uh ... well, you see,' I stammered, trying to come up with a coherent response. 'It's just that ... My dad's been busy with his work, and I didn't want to bother him. I promise he wouldn't mind.'

I understood that we were years apart in age, but in just three weeks' time I would be eighteen and most definitely could make my own choices about where I go and with who.

'Teenagers are the same all over the world,' Folake said, laughing at my poor attempt at an excuse.

Relief washed over me as I realised she wasn't judging me or angry. 'Yeah, well, I guess I just wanted a bit of an escape, you know? Things have been a bit complicated lately.'

And just like that, I found myself opening up to her about everything that had happened since my dad left for Nigeria. I shared the whirlwind of emotions I'd been experiencing, from my confusing friendship with Sinéad, the unexpected kiss with Jack, the uncertain nature of Clara, the creeping anxiety of going to college soon and the mixed feelings it had all stirred up.

As I spoke, I realised how freeing it was to have someone to confide in who didn't particularly know those involved.

Folake listened patiently, occasionally interrupting to ask thoughtful questions or give encouraging responses. It was as if the act of sharing my thoughts aloud was helping me process them and gain a clearer perspective on my own feelings.

This must be how people who go to therapy feel.

When I finally finished recounting my story, I let out a deep breath, feeling lighter as if a weight had been lifted off my shoulders.

'Wow,' Folake said, her voice still gentle. 'You've been through quite a lot in such a short time. From the sounds of it, you needed to let it all out.'

I nodded, happy to see she understood. 'Yeah, I just … I don't know what to make of everything. It's like I'm stuck in this confusing web of questions and uncertainties.'

Folake smiled warmly, her eyes offering reassurance. 'Life has a way of throwing us curve balls, Abi. You'll find your way through it. Sometimes, all we need is a bit of time and perspective.'

This sounded like a more mature version of what Clara was trying to tell me.

'So, do you think I should talk to Sinéad again?' I asked her, wanting a bit more guidance on the matter.

Folake leaned back in her chair, letting the sun warm her face. 'Communication is key in any friendship and relationship. If something is bothering you, it's important to address it. But remember, timing matters too. Be calm and open to all possibilities when you go to talk to her.'

I picked up a strand of Folake's hair and started braiding it. 'I think you're right! I should at least hear what she has to say for herself, but I'm scared.'

'Give your friendship the chance it deserves,' Folake advised. 'Things aren't always as they seem.'

We continued our conversation as I worked on Folake's hair, discussing everything from her own teenage friend-ship dramas to my cravings for Nigerian dishes. She even promised to whip up some of them when I dropped by next time. The sun began to dip lower in the sky, casting a warm, golden glow over the garden.

Finally, I was on the last braid, letting out a sigh of relief.

'Ta-da! All done!' I announced, stretching my fingers that had gotten a bit cramped.

I stepped back, taking in my handiwork with a sense of pride. Each line of cornrows was perfectly symmetrical and neatly aligned. I couldn't help but feel a surge of satisfaction at the sight of my work.

With all the juice from earlier, my bladder was also now demanding my attention and I needed to run to the bathroom.

'It's the second door in the hallway, just under the stairs,' Folake directed.

'Thanks! I'll be right back.'

Walking down the hallway, I stopped to take in the vibrant artwork on the wall. I made a note to ask Folake if she'd painted it.

I entered the bathroom and took a moment to look at myself in the mirror. My reflection showed a girl who had been through a lot in the past few days, but also a girl who was starting to feel better. I smiled and my reflection smiled back at me.

As I washed my hands and splashed some water on my face, I thought about what Folake had said. Communication, timing and being open to all possibilities. It all made sense, and I realised that I needed to approach my future conversation with Sinéad with an open heart and mind. Maybe I overreacted and it wasn't what it looked like at all.

I didn't return directly to the kitchen; curiosity got the better of me. The door across from the bathroom was slightly open and the lights were on. I wanted to see what the interior looked like.

I opened the door a bit more and peeked my head in. The room was small; a large desk and chair sat in the centre, scattered with sketches and papers. This must be her home office. The walls were covered with colour swatches, sketches, and interior mood boards, highlighting a project she must currently be working on. A small shelf was lined with design books, trinkets, and even more art supplies filled the space.

I opened the door more and stepped inside. It reminded me of the Art Room at St Enda's, vibrant and chaotic. On another wall, there was a corkboard filled with Polaroid pictures, postcards, and little notes.

I knew I shouldn't have, but I wanted to see where the postcards were from, so I moved closer. The postcards showcased a variety of places: the Eiffel Tower in Paris, a colourful market in Marrakesh and the serene beaches of Bali.

Then I looked closer at the Polaroids, most of which showed a gathering of people at what looked like a wedding.

My gaze lingered on one picture in particular. Folake was holding a bouquet of flowers. She wore a flowing white silk dress with delicate spaghetti straps. Instead of a traditional veil, a regal silver crown adorned her afro. She stood beneath a flower arch.

It wasn't just Folake's wedding look that captivated me, it was the presence of the older man beside her. He stood there in a cream-coloured suit, smiling with pride, his arm firmly wrapped around Folake's waist. His eyes, thin but piercing, stared back at me as though he knew what I was thinking.

He always knew what I was thinking. This was my dad.

CHAPTER TWENTY- ONE

IN ANOTHER LIFE

My heart pounded in my chest as I stared at the picture. My mind couldn't fully process what I was seeing. It couldn't be a coincidence. There was my dad, standing beside Folake on what appeared to be their wedding day. The realisation that my dad had kept such a massive secret from me was like a punch to the gut.

All the pieces started to fall into place. Folake wasn't just a stranger who had liked a picture on my Instagram page. She knew *exactly* who I was. She must have, and she'd been pretending not to this entire time. She purposely didn't mention that she was married. Married to *my dad*.

When did all of this even happen and why didn't *he* tell me? My mind raced with questions, each one more over-whelming than the last.

I stumbled out of the room, my heart pounding in my ears. I could hear Folake's footsteps getting closer. She was in the kitchen now.

'You OK, Abi?'

Her voice sounded like it was ringing in my head. I felt so exposed, so weak.

I just stood in the hallway, which Folake was now also in. Her expression changed from concern to confusion she looked to the open door of her office and then to me. It still hadn't clicked.

'Abi, what's going on? You look like you've seen a ghost.'

I still just stood there, shaking my head, struggling to find the words to explain, but I needed to know for sure. 'In your office, I saw my dad. In a picture. You and my dad ...' My voice trembled with every word.

Her eyes widened in surprise, as if she hadn't expected me to find out or make the connection on my own. She took a step towards me, trying to compose herself, carefully thinking about her next words. 'Abi, I ... I didn't want you to find out like this.'

'Is *this* why you've been asking me to talk to my dad ... because of this?' my voice wavered as I fought to hold back angry tears. I felt pathetic.

Folake sighed, her shoulders slumping slightly. 'Yes, Abi, I didn't want to get too close to you before he had a chance to explain.'

'Why didn't you *tell* me?' I managed to choke out. 'Why didn't *Dad* tell me?'

Folake's eyes met mine, her expression pained. 'Abi, I know this is a lot to take in. I wanted to give your dad the chance to talk to you himself, I didn't think it was my place, I didn't want to overstep ...'

The weight of her words hung heavy in the air, but only one question sprang to mind.

'How long ...' I wasn't even able to get the big 'M word' out.

'Your dad and I got married in Nigeria last year, he told me about you and wanted to wait till he felt you were ready to meet me.'

They had been married for *A YEAR*!

My anger was still bubbling just beneath the surface, and I couldn't hold it back any longer. 'So, you both decided it was better to just keep me in the dark ... that's evil.' Embarrassment crept in, making me question if I should have seen the signs, if I was too naive or trusting. I felt foolish, tricked, like a pawn in some elaborate game that I never signed up for.

Folake's face twisted in anguish, her hands reaching out to me, but I sidestepped her touch. 'Abi, I didn't want it to be like this. When you came up on my Instagram, I didn't even realise I had liked your picture, I didn't want to hurt you or have things get complicated like this, but when you followed me and messaged, you seemed so sweet and seemed like you needed someone to talk to. I shouldn't have encouraged it or even messaged back, but ...'

'Hurt me? It's a bit too late!' I scoffed, feeling a bitter laugh escape my lips. 'So, when I was telling you about my life ...you didn't think you could have mentioned it then? Or were you just secretly practising to be my mom?' Even saying it made me wince in disgust. I couldn't believe I told this woman, this stranger, so much about myself while she looked me in the eye and pretended to know nothing.

The memories of our conversations replayed in my mind, and I couldn't shake the feeling that everything I shared with Folake, every piece of myself I exposed, was now tainted. I questioned if Folake genuinely cared about me or if our interactions were nothing more than a calculated act. Did she ever like me for me, or was I just a means to an end, a way for her to gather information for my dad?

Folake's shoulders slumped, and her voice was soft, heavy with guilt. 'Abi, I know how it all sounds, I got too excited when you reached out and I wasn't thinking logically. I had heard so many wonderful things about you from Deji, I mean your dad. Then meeting you for coffee was so wonderful so when you reached out again ... anyway, it doesn't matter now, I'm completely at fault, I shouldn't have rushed it.'

My anger was tinged with sorrow now. The woman I had come to trust, the one who had offered me advice and a listening ear, had kept this life-altering truth hidden. How could I have been so blind? Was it so easy for Folake to deceive me, to pretend to be a friend while hiding such a monumental secret?

My dad was just as guilty. He had built an entire life outside of me. It felt like the ground beneath me was shifting.

I turned away from Folake, my fists clenched at my sides. 'I can't be here anymore ...' I said, on the verge of breaking down there and then.

Folake just nodded. She couldn't say anything to redeem herself and I wasn't ready to listen to anything else she had to say. This truth had broken my ability to trust even my own family, let alone this woman.

I walked and I walked and I walked until eventually my surroundings shifted. The charm of Lahinch faded into the background, replaced by the steady hum of the motorway and swaying trees.

As the distance grew between me and Folake's house, all I felt now was a deep ache of hurt. I had considered Folake a friend, someone I could confide in and trust, but it was my dad's role in all this that pained me the most. I felt the loss of a version of my dad that I thought I knew.

The traffic rushed past, and I had to sit under a bus shelter to steady my breath.

Breathe, Abi. Breathe.

Tears built up in my eyes for the second time that week and I felt an overwhelming sense of loneliness. I wiped away the tears with the back of my hand, my gaze shifting from the passing cars to the evening sky above. Everything felt so uncertain, much like my own future. It was clear that things would never go back to being the way they were.

My phone vibrated in my pocket, jarring me from my thoughts. Dad was calling. I would have to confront him eventually, but for now, all I could do was focus on breathing and on putting one foot in front of the other.

I only needed one thing right now and that was my best friend.

CHAPTER TWENTY-TWO

SILLY GOOSE

'You look awful,' was the first thing Sinéad blurted out as I stumbled through the door of the launderette. 'What's going on? I've been calling your phone! I've been worried about you, I even considered storming your house,' Sinéad exclaimed.

I let out a shaky breath, feeling a lump forming in my throat. 'It's ... it's a long story,' I managed to say, my voice betraying the tears I had been shedding.

Sinéad's expression softened, and she pulled me into a comforting hug. 'Well, I've got time. Spill the beans.'

I hesitated for a moment, struggling to find the right words to begin. 'Dad ... he's got a wife,' I finally blurted out, realising that diving into the heart of the matter was the only way to start.

Sinéad's eyebrows shot up in surprise. 'Wait, *what*? Your dad has a *wife*? Since when?'

I sank into a chair at the back of the launderette, feeling drained from the hour-long walk along the motorway into town. Sinéad joined me, waiting for an explanation.

'I found out today. I was at Folake's place, a lady I met at Ryan's Café, well, I met her first online. Anyway, it turns out she's ... she's my dad's wife.'

Sinéad's jaw dropped. She was stunned trying to keep up with the story.

'*What?* Hold on, back up. So, this Folake woman you met on the internet is *married to your dad?* How do you know for sure? Did you ask your dad?'

'I don't have to, I saw their wedding picture in her house and Dad has been calling me on the phone since,' I said, pulling out my phone to show her the thirteen missed calls from his number.

Sinéad's eyes widened with disbelief. 'Abi, that's ... that's crazy. Why would your dad keep something like this from you?'

I shrugged helplessly, searching for the answer to that question myself. 'I don't know, Sinéad. I'm just ... I'm so angry and confused right now. Everything's a mess.'

Sinéad put her arm around me, offering comfort. 'I can't even imagine how you're feeling right now. But one thing's for sure, you need to talk to your dad. Get his side of the story.'

'Are you dating Jack?' I asked. I didn't mean to blurt it out so abruptly, but it was still a pressing thought in my mind and since today was all about uncovering truths, I might as well know now.

Sinéad's eyes widened in surprise at my sudden change of topic and then she burst into laughter, she seemed amused. 'Me? DATE JACK? Have you gone mad?'

Why was she laughing at me, couldn't she see that I was being dead serious? I know what I saw.

'I was coming to see you the other day, but instead I caught you both outside here, laughing, then you hugged, and you looked super happy about it,' I explained, feeling a bit awkward now that I admitted I was spying on them.

Sinéad continued to chuckle, shaking her head. 'Oh, Abi, you've got quite the imagination. Trust me, there's nothing romantic between Jack and me. He was asking me where he should take you on a date and I made a joke about him messing it all up since it would be his first time actually trying to impress a girl. The hug was friendly. I was laughing and smiling at the idea of both of ye being so nervous when it's so obvious there's something there …'

Realisation hit me like a ton of bricks. I had let my assumptions get the best of me, and in the process, I could have damaged my friendship with Sinéad. I felt a pang of regret for not trusting her and for not giving her a chance to explain. I also didn't know whether to mention I had accidentally started a false rumour about this in Clara's circle.

'I'm so sorry, Sinéad,' I said sheepishly. 'I shouldn't have assumed things without asking you first... but you were avoiding me, and I figured that was the reason.'

Sinéad's expression softened, and she reached out to place a reassuring hand on my shoulder. 'You're right, I've been avoiding you because I didn't want my own issues to ruin your joy. The truth is, I've been feeling pretty down and sad about everyone else heading off to college soon, we both know I'll be stuck here doing the same old things for God knows how long.'

She sighed. 'I ran into one of the girls from my art class when I was at Electric. She'll be applying for a scholarship to the National College of Art and Design, and I swear it, she can't even draw a straight line. It just hit me that I never even considered that as an option for myself because you know ... I've haven't got as many coins in my piggy bank.'

I hadn't thought of it like that, I'd been thinking Sinéad just didn't care about school and college. I had been so caught up in my own world that I hadn't even realised that she too might be struggling with thoughts of the future.

'I didn't know you felt like this ... and for what it's worth, if anyone should be going to art school, it's you, your lines are very, very straight,' I said, making us both laugh.

I knew that no matter where life takes us, I definitely didn't want to ever lose Sinéad as a friend.

'Abi, you do seriously need to talk to your dad … maybe when you get some answers, all of this won't seem so bad?' she said, reminding me of the other big mess in my life that I still had to deal with. I doubted her words, but I nodded my head to show that I was listening.

Sinéad patted my back. 'Whatever happens, remember that I'm always here for you, just answer your phone next time, you silly goose.'

As we sat there in the launderette, I felt grateful for Sinéad's tenderness. No matter how tangled things got, her presence always made them a little more bearable.

CHAPTER TWENTY-THREE

LOOSE CURLS

I was huddled under Sinéad's cosy duvet, the room fully in darkness. She had fallen asleep next to me a while ago, but my mind was still racing.

My phone became the only source of light as Dad's messages came in. I couldn't help but read each one. My finger hovered over my phone's screen, scrolling up and down.

Dad:

'I never meant for any of this to hurt you. I should have told you the truth from the beginning. I love you, Abi. I hope you can find it in your heart to forgive me.'

Then a picture popped up – it was an online booking confirming a one-way flight back to Ireland. He was coming back sooner than expected, tomorrow night to be exact.

Dad:

'Abi, I'm on my way back – it's an eight-hour flight. We need to talk. I'm so sorry for not being upfront with you about everything. I know you're hurt, and I can't even imagine how you're feeling right now. Please let me explain.'

I looked at Sinéad. I was jealous of her being able to find peace in sleep. My phone buzzed again, another message from Dad. This time, I just silenced it and put it under my pillow.

The smell of sizzling bacon tickled my nose, inviting me to wake up. Two pale legs stood in front of me. I looked up to see Margaret with her sleeping baby on her shoulder. She was holding a plate full of mouthwatering bacon, eggs and toast. Her hair was tied back and her face stern.

'Sinéad sent this up for you ... she's on breakfast duty,' Margaret announced, her expression as no-nonsense as ever. Even though she was just a little bit older than us, she liked to remind us of her seniority, even in her body language, which Sinéad and I never really took seriously.

'Thanks,' I mumbled, rubbing my eyes to shake off the last remnants of sleep dust.

Sinéad must have figured that I wasn't in the mood for a cheerful breakfast gathering, which would be correct. I could hear the chatter and laughter of her family downstairs. My phone now showed four more notifications from my dad, a reminder of the conversation I was avoiding.

Even though I didn't feel super hungry, my stomach grumbled as the delicious smell of the fried food got to me. I realised I had not eaten since yesterday afternoon. I took another glance at my phone – it showed that it was already noon.

I dragged myself out of the comfort of Sinéad's bed and eventually started making my way back home, hoping to avoid any familiar faces. Earlier, I caught a glimpse of myself in the mirror. I really did look awful.

My braids were now matted and frizzy, dark bags had taken up space under my eyes and my skin had lost its usual glow, leaving me looking pale and worn out.

I took another nap when I got home, my body was begging me to catch up on much-needed rest. By the time I peeled my eyes open for the second time that day, the sun was already setting. I calculated that Dad would be back maybe after midnight, if there were no delays to his flight. At least now with all the extra sleep, I had some energy to deal with his return.

The weight of my braids was starting to feel uncomfortable and annoying, especially when brushed against my neck and face. I realised my hair tools were still back at Folake's place, on the garden table to be exact. Forgotten in the madness of everything that had happened.

Feeling irritated by the length of my hair, I knew I needed to take my braids out, I couldn't bear it any longer.

I didn't want to be the Abi who had meticulously put these braids in, and I definitely didn't want to look like her. My thoughts were impulsive, but I just allowed them to lead me to the kitchen, I didn't want to think it through.

I grabbed a pair of scissors, my heart racing. With a deep breath, I began to snip away at the long braids from the nape of my neck, watching as each strand fell to the floor. I knew I was cutting some inches off my natural hair, and it would now be shorter too. At this moment, I just didn't care.

Using a fork as a makeshift rat-tail comb, I began the process of unravelling each braid. Sitting on the kitchen floor, surrounded by a growing pile of crumpled hair extensions, I worked for what felt like hours. The repetitive motion of untangling the hair became relaxing and as the braids came undone, I felt as if I was letting go of something deeper.

In the shower, I took my time washing my hair, the warm water soothing against my scalp. I let the water beat down on my head, lathering soap and massaging it gently to cleanse away the dirt residue. I watched the suds swirl and disappear down the drain. As I rinsed the soap away, I felt a sense of lightness.

I wiped the fogged-up bathroom mirror and came face to face with my transformed reflection. My hair now rested just below my ears, the tight curls forming their own pattern around my face. I looked more like Mom than I ever had before and for a moment, I felt like she was actually staring back at me too.

CHAPTER TWENTY-FOUR

OUT OF MY BUBBLE

'Abi! Abi!' Dad shouted as he rushed into the house that night. I was waiting patiently in the living room. I purposely stayed up and left the lights on to let him know I was very much still awake. I was ready.

He looked like he hadn't had much sleep, his shirt unusually creased and bunched up. His eyes were puffy and red.

The first thing he did was pull me in for an unreturned hug, kneeling in front of me while I sat on the sofa. He might as well have been embracing a sack of potatoes.

'Why didn't you *tell* me, Dad?' I asked. I had played out all the potential ways this scenario could go, I had thought of all the ways I could ask the same questions, I was prepared to hear what his excuse could be. 'Why did you keep it a secret?'

He got up from the floor and plopped himself beside me on the sofa. I moved further down, wanting to maintain the physical distance.

'It's a long story, Abi,' he said, his face now in the palm of his hands as though he was hiding his shame. 'Folake and I met in Nigeria on my first work trip with the company. She was designing some of the office spaces for the new hires. We connected and things just ... progressed. We got to know each other better ... we liked each other, but I didn't plan for it to turn into something serious.'

I stared at him, slightly disgusted at the thought of my forty-six-year-old dad even dating, but I wanted him to continue explaining himself. 'But then, why did you get married ... there and not here? Like, that's a really weird thing to do, Dad. That's a big decision to make. Then you come back and act like everything is normal. You know this isn't normal, right?'

Dad sighed deeply; he looked like he was physically in pain, his face heavy with guilt. 'I know it's a strange thing to do, but it made so much sense too. I can't explain it the way I want to, I just didn't want to force you to move on ... especially with everything that's happened ... with your mom passing ...'

I was speechless. Move on? Why would we move on? Moving on implied letting go of someone or something. My frustration bubbled up again.

'So, what you're saying is you've moved on from Mom and you felt I wasn't "moving on" fast enough?' I said angrily.

Dad reached out and placed a hand on my shoulder. I shrugged it off.

'*Omo mi,*' he said in Yoruba; this meant 'my child.' 'I loved your mom so deeply; she will always be in my heart.' Dad's eyes met mine, his expression intensified. 'I can't replace her; I would never want to. What I feel for Folake doesn't change that.'

My anger was burning now, and my voice got louder, bolder. 'But you're still moving on, starting a new life without her … without *me*.'

Dad took my hand in his, firmly holding it so I couldn't pull away. 'No, I didn't plan for this to happen. It's not about replacing your mom or you. You'll forever be a part of me! I was waiting to tell you after your birthday. I didn't want anything to distract you from school, from your exams.'

As his words settled, I noticed the sincerity in his eyes. Dad had carried the weight of his decision, thinking it was the best way to keep me focused on my education, as warped as it may be.

I turned away, struggling to contain my tears. 'It's just... it's all so much.'

'I know, my daughter. I understand that you're hurting. I should have talked to you sooner.' His voice quietened as though he was thinking of his next words carefully. 'I suppose I should tell you this now too.'

I looked at him, wondering what more life-altering news there possibly could be to tell.

'One of the reasons I asked Folake to move here a few months ago is so that she can get to know the healthcare system … because she's going to have a baby … you're going to be a big sister!' he said, delicately allowing each word to land in the air.

This knocked the wind out of me.

I stared at my dad, my mind struggling to process the new information he had just dropped on me. Folake didn't even look pregnant. Surely I would have noticed this.

A sister? A baby? It felt like my world had been turned upside down yet again, and I wasn't sure how to react.

'Are you serious?' I finally managed to say in disbelief, but of course I knew he was, he wouldn't say it if it wasn't true. 'Where is everyone going to live? When is Folake due? Where will the baby sleep?'

The questions spilled out, my attempt to make sense of the new reality that was unfolding.

Dad, sensing my confusion, took a deep breath before answering, 'Those are all very big question. The answer to the biggest one is Folake is due in four months.'

'So, this was your plan all along? Wait till you can ship me off to college and move *her* in so you can play happy family with your new wife. And to think I was actually coming around to understanding your secret marriage, and now you drop this bomb on me?' The words tumbled out like venom.

Could it be that I had intentionally only seen what I wanted to see all this time? A flashback returned me to Ryan's Café. When there was only one ring on Folake's hand, I remembered it now, sparkling when she lifted her cup to her mouth. Then when we were in her house, I had thought I noticed a slight bulge in her stomach. Yes, I did; when she was in the hallway, she had her hand pressed against her stomach.

Everything felt connected. My ability to only see what I wanted to see. I never wanted to know why Dad would hide in his office to make calls during the weekends. I never fully questioned that Sinéad might actually care about going to college. I never paid attention to Jack when he made sure to greet me most mornings when he passed my locker at St Enda's. I had been living in my own bubble, waiting for people to make things blatantly obvious to me. I felt like for the first time, I was awake, finally seeing things for what they really were.

My dad's words about him wanting to pick the right time to tell me about the marriage and the baby echoed in my mind. Would there ever have been a right time?

BRAIDS TAKE A DAY

As I looked at my dad in confusion, it struck me that I had been so focused on my own concerns and plans that I hadn't fully considered that he might also be looking towards the future.

Once I left for college, I wouldn't just be leaving behind my childhood home and memories. I would no longer be the thing that kept my dad anchored to this place.

For years, it had been just the two of us, navigating life together. But now, with Folake in his life and a new baby on the way, he was moving forward too. He had his own life to live, his own dreams to chase, and this was the start of it.

CHAPTER TWENTY-FIVE

SPECIAL DELIVERY

The following few days were tense, to say the least.

My dad and I moved around the house like two strangers sharing a space, only exchanging simple pleasantries like 'Good morning' and 'thanks.'

Dad was trying to be attentive while giving me the room I needed. He would knock on my door, peeping in to check that I was still in bed, since I barely made any noise. He would sometimes bring a cup of tea, a glass of water or just simply ask if I was OK.

He knew I wanted to be alone, but he couldn't help but make sure I wasn't forgetting to eat.

Even though the wounds ran deep, the rawness of my emotions was finally easing up. Maybe it was my brain giving in after the many bouts of breaking news, but I found myself occasionally wondering what it would be like to have Folake around. After all, she was very likeable and calming to be around. I could see why my dad was drawn to her.

Then there was that other part of me that just could not forgive them for their deception, even if they felt their reasons were justified. Trust had been shattered, and the debris of their deception surrounded me. Yet, another part of me, maybe driven by a longing for something that felt like a full family, the type you see smiling around a TV in a Christmas ad, entertained the notion of forgiveness.

As if I already didn't have enough on my plate, I was also mentally trying to bring order to the other parts of my life.

I had declined multiple invitations from Sinéad to meet up and once I filled her in on all the new developments, she fully understood. She even cheekily asked, 'Is our new stepmom hot?'

I didn't reply; the answer, though, was obvious.

I had distanced myself from the group chat with Clara, Niamh and Shauna, but I was texting Clara separately. Without the others, she was easy to talk to.

I was starting to realise that without the dynamics and hierarchy that came with being students of St Enda's, we all had the option to start afresh and settle into who we wanted to be, and I hoped that Niamh and Shauna would also come to that realisation soon.

I ended up explaining to Clara the mistake I made when I told her that Sinéad and Jack were together. I was glad to have set things right and corrected my own exaggerated assumption. I just hoped Clara didn't tell anyone else about the misunderstanding. I didn't want to get on Sinéad's bad side after everything that had happened.

Just mind yourself, Abi,' Clara texted back.

It was kind of funny; the more I got to know Clara, the more I saw the similarities between Clara and Sinéad. Sure, they both rocked these tough exteriors, but it didn't take long to realise that behind those seemingly iron gates, there was a whole lot of softness and heart. Turns out, we are more than our first impressions suggest.

The doorbell rang downstairs. It was probably Ms Kelly coming to welcome Dad back since the three weeks he was supposed to be away had finally come to an end. She would have had no way of knowing about his early return. We've both been inside, healing within the walls of our house.

Since my impulsive haircut, I braided my hair again, this time using only my natural hair. The style mimicked a braided bob, with my curls loose at the ends of each braid. It was carefree and lightweight, just what I needed at this time.

Dad commented on my new hairstyle, saying it made me look 'creative and cool'. I smiled awkwardly, appreciating his compliment, but also not wanting it to open up new conversations. I was OK with the eggshells we were both walking on, at least for now.

Strangely, it wasn't Ms Kelly's voice I heard from downstairs. The voice was low and clear, but I knew for certain who it belonged to. It was Jack.

Startled, I jumped out of my bed, my pyjamas still marked with splotches of hot chocolate and crumbs from the jam sandwich that Dad had brought up for lunch. Jack's unexpected presence was a shock, he was the only person I had intentionally not followed up with. I was convinced I had missed my chance and he had probably lost interest, but clearly, this boy was determined.

In a panic, I looked around my room for a clean shirt to change int. I also grabbed the nearest pair of leggings I could find. I hoped I looked somewhat presentable. If we were going to have a hard conversation, I might as well look ready for it.

While I changed, Dad's voice bellowed up the stairs, calling for me to come and greet my guest.

I wiped the crumbs from my face and hastily threw a jumper over my top. I then applied some lip gloss I found within arm's reach. I tried so hard to not look frazzled as I walked down the stairs, avoiding my dad's questioning eyes completely. Was this his worst nightmare? Having a boy call round for me?

In this scenario, we were the same, we both had our secrets, and I wasn't going to feel guilty for mine.

When I reached the bottom of the stairs, I saw Jack standing by the door, holding the largest bouquet of flowers I had ever seen. It was a glorious arrangement of yellow sunflowers, pastel pink roses and blue hydrangeas. I was taken aback and unsure of what to say or do next.

As I stood there, caught off guard by his unexpected presence as well as the grand display of affection, Jack just stood there sheepishly grinning waiting for me to say something. Once he realised my speechless state, he took the lead.

'Hi, Abi,' Jack said. He seemed nervous. It was strange to watch as he shifted his weight from one foot to another. Was he intimidated by my father's presence? I would be too.

'Hey,' I managed to reply, my voice coming out a bit more breathless than I intended. I could feel my cheeks warming up. I bit my lip and hid my obvious delight.

'These are for you,' Jack said, holding out the bouquet for me to take. His hands were shaking so much that he nearly dropped them. The flowers seemed too large compared to my shorter, smaller arms, but I didn't care. I took them and held them close.

'Thank you,' I said softly, my fingers brushing against the rose petals as I held them.

Dad cleared his throat, breaking the brief silence between us. He looked puzzled, and I knew he so badly wanted to stop what he was witnessing.

Jack continued, 'I umm, came round to ask you … I mean your dad, if I could take you to the Debs, that is … if you want to go!'

'Umm,' was all I could muster. There had been so much on my mind that I hadn't even thought about the Debs ball in August.

Sinéad and I had agreed that if we were to go, we would be each other's date, but it really wasn't that important to us. Between the event, the dress and all the glam involved with it, I knew it was very expensive for her and I didn't want her to feel bad about that, so I had told her I was just going to ask Dad to put the money towards my college accommodation.

'Hmm,' Dad muttered, interrupting again. I knew he'd have questions, but he was holding it all in. If things weren't as they were between us, I'm sure he would have shown his stricter side. Instead, he just turned around and walked towards his office and he left his door slightly open. I didn't doubt that he was still listening.

It was now just Jack and me alone in the hallway.

Finally feeling a bit more at ease, Jack let out a sigh of relief. 'Abi, I've been trying to get in touch with you, to clear things up… Sinéad came round to Vinny's and told me about the misunderstanding.'

'Oh, you must think I'm such a fool …' I replied.

'No … I really don't. After Electric, I started overthinking the date I promised to take you on, I wanted to do something memorable. So, I went to ask Sinéad what you like and where you'd like to go.' Jack chuckled nervously, running a hand through his beautiful hair. I wanted to reach out and do the same.

'Now I feel like I should have just asked you yourself and avoided this whole mess. I'm just not great at this sort of thing …' he said.

From where I stood, he was doing a great job of explaining his perspective. I looked down at the bouquet of flowers in my hands, the biggest smile on my face. From Sinéad's explanation about their conversation, to what Jack was saying, it all made sense.

'You don't even have to explain, it all my fault, but thank you for coming over,' I said, finally looking back up at Jack. 'And thank you for the flowers, they're perfect.'

Jack smiled back. He looked so handsome, the butterflies in my belly were dancing around with glee.

'Now that that's out of the way, how do you feel about that date or the Debs?' Jack said.

I took a deep breath, feeling the weight of the world

on my shoulders. 'I'd like that but …' I was hesitant as my cheeks and ears were warm and tingly.

I liked Jack, I really did, but I still felt terrible for the way I spiralled and let my imagination get the better of me. What if that happened again?

Jack's smile faded slightly; he was trying to hide the disappointment in his eyes. 'But what?'

I hesitated again, taking another long pause. I just needed to be honest, the same way he was with me. 'Jack, I really like you, but there's a lot going on in my life right now, and I'm a complete mess …' I sounded so mature and confident; I was impressed with myself.

Jack's expression softened. 'Abi, I don't expect you to have your life together if that's what you're thinking, but I also don't want to rush you into anything you're not ready for. I've liked you for longer than you realise, so I don't mind waiting for when you feel ready. I'm still around if you change your mind …'

How did I get so lucky to have a boy who was so understanding and patient at my door?

'You're really amazing, you know that?' I said.

Jack, with a touch of humour, added, 'I'm not sure if it matters now, but your good friend Sinéad told me you love Italian food. There's a new place in Ennis that apparently makes their pasta from scratch … I'm just throwing that out there.'

I smiled at this. He really had given this first date thing a lot of thought and a part of me couldn't help but consider it again. Placing the flowers on the floor beside me, I took a step towards him. On his warm cheek, I planted a gentle kiss.

As I did this, I wrapped my arms around his neck, and he responded by wrapping his arms around my waist. The warmth of the moment enveloped us, and for a while, the world outside seemed to fade away.

While letting go I said, 'I guess Italian doesn't sound so bad.'

He wasn't expecting it and grinned so that all his teeth could be seen. He had that lopsided smile that I had grown to like.

'Well, let me know when you're ready,' Jack said. It felt like this time, the ball was fully in my court.

As the conversation lingered, I thought about all the things this summer had already taught me about myself and how much I had changed in these few weeks.

While I still did not have all the answers about my changing family or my future, I was ready to embrace whatever came my way and decide what I wanted for myself. No matter how difficult that was.

CHAPTER TWENTY-SIX

TREASURES

The decision to invite Folake over for dinner was a spur-of-the-moment idea that took even Dad by surprise. As the words slipped out of my mouth I noticed the subtle shift in Dad's expression, his raised eyebrows and the slight parting of his lips.

I wanted to get past the hard conversations we all needed to have and since Jack's visit, I felt a little joy creep back in, a little more optimism and hope. Truthfully, I felt like I could take on the world.

Surprisingly, Dad didn't press me about Jack coming to the door. All he did was ask if he was a 'classmate' from St Enda's, to which I nodded. There was no need for me to say more.

Dad even helped me find a vase big enough for the flowers. I placed it in the centre of the table where we would all gather later for dinner that evening.

There were other things buzzing around in my head that I needed to get off my chest. As mad as I was, Dad and Folake were already married and it was too late for that to change. I could work on accepting that ... very slowly. What was bothering me though was that I was slowly starting to feel myself get a little excited about the whole baby situation, a little person that would arrive and take up space.

A tiny human who would grow up with thoughts and emotions. One day this baby would be a teenager who would walk in the same streets that I do now. Despite all the craziness, there was a thread connecting me and this baby.

With two more months left in the house and my eighteenth birthday in a week's time, I was also thinking more and more about whether I even wanted to study nursing in Dublin.

Truth be told, I had absolutely no passion for it, I was only doing it because it made Dad happy. But lately, I found myself questioning whether I should just go after what truly sparked something in me, what made me genuinely happy.

And, surprise, surprise, that something was hair.

Folake unknowingly planted the seed, and it had been growing steadily ever since. The idea of pursuing what genuinely interested me felt like a breath of fresh air in a life that often felt scripted. Hair – who would've thought?

Anne came early to start her usual cleaning round, but with us both being home, there wasn't really much for her to do. From the way she was analysing us, I felt she could sense the shift in the house.

I confirmed it when I asked Dad, in front of her, if we could work together to clear out some of Mom's things from the spare room. While Dad seemed hesitant, he agreed and mumbled something about having to unpack his own suitcase so he wouldn't be able to help. I think the truth is, as much as he'd like to think he has, there are parts of him that still haven't moved on.

I didn't want Mom to be a thing of the past, her life with us hidden away within four walls. I wanted to sift through her stuff and have parts of her in the now.

Thankfully, Anne wasn't her usual grumpy self during the task. She helped me sort through each box, cleaning years of lingering dust off untouched items.

We separated things into two piles – the ones that were meant for charity and the ones I had an eye on.

Although I wasn't the same size as Mom, I had a secret hope that maybe one day some of her dresses would fit me. As I went through the boxes, I stumbled upon a collection of accessories and hats. They were like hidden treasures, outdated ones, but valuable all the same. I didn't know how yet, but I'd find a way to blend them into my own style.

'Your dad has done a great job with you,' Anne said, watching me carefully flip through some of my baby pictures in one of the boxes.

I looked up from the box, surprised by her words. Anne wasn't one to offer compliments freely, she mostly seemed annoyed by everything. So, I took it that she really meant what she was saying.

'Yeah, he's tried his best,' I replied, smiling.

It was true. Even though Dad could be strict at times he had always done everything he could for me. He was my rock and anyone who knew us could see that.

Anne's expression softened, and I caught a glimpse of something more in her eyes. For a brief second, the toughness seemed to melt away, but just as quickly, she turned her attention back to wiping down something in her hands.

I turned my focus back to the pictures and held one of them up. It was of Mom and Dad wearing Christmas jumpers, holding a toddler version of me up with pride. I was caught mid-laugh, chubby cheeks and wide eyes, completely oblivious to the pile of presents scattered around us. It captured a moment of pure happiness and love.

I didn't doubt that Dad truly loved Mom, the same way I never needed to doubt that he loved me. I decided that when Folake arrived, I'd keep an open mind.

Dinner time came around and I truly have never seen Dad so stylishly dressed. He had trimmed his beard and was wearing a freshly ironed navy button-up shirt with white denim shorts. He even had on his watch and a simple gold necklace. Was this how he dressed for dates? It was so different to how he dressed for school meetings or work events.

He couldn't sit still as we waited for Folake to arrive. He even went as far as to prepare a traditional Nigerian dish called asaro, made of yam, plantain and meat cooked in a hearty blend of spices and palm oil. He was already using some of the ingredients he had just brought back from Nigeria.

The kitchen was filled with the yummy smells of home cooking. My stomach growled with hunger thanks to all the work Anne and I put into clearing up the spare room which now looked more spacious than ever.

Dad practically sprinted to the door when Folake arrived. He was like a nervous schoolboy, it was really strange to see him so flustered and giddy.

It dawned on me that for the first time, I was going to be seeing them together. It was too late to turn back now. She was already entering the house.

Folake, glamorous as ever, sashayed in with a warm smile. She too seemed nervous.

She was dressed in a vibrant, purple knee-length dress and a little head scarf wrapped stylishly around her head while her short braids fell around her face. This time, I looked to see if there was a bulge in her stomach.

It was there, small, but it was there.

'Dinner smells good, Deji,' Folake said as she greeted Dad. They hugged then Folake kissed Dad on the cheek. 'I'm glad you're finally back!' she said.

They seemed conscious that I was watching them like a hawk, and I couldn't hide it. This was something I hadn't seen in Dad's life for ages. It was like watching a whole new episode of his world unfold.

Seated around the table, you could cut the tension with a knife. I played with my food. It was delicious, but my thoughts were everywhere else. My fork clinking on the plate felt like a drumbeat for the unspoken issues hanging in the air.

Folake tried to break the ice, looking at me and saying, 'You look good. I really like what you've done with your hair.' It was a small peace offering, I guess. I gave a nod, appreciating the attempt to make things less awkward.

Dad and Folake looked good together. Like a power couple fit for magazine covers. As I sat there, my mind brought me back to the picture of their wedding day. I couldn't help but wonder about the details that surrounded the event that I wasn't a part of.

How long did it take to plan? Were both sides of their families there, celebrating their love? Did Folake have bridesmaids? Was there a theme? I imagined the vibrant colours, the traditional attire, and the joyous atmosphere of a Nigerian wedding.

But among those thoughts, the one question that wouldn't go away was how did my dad feel, knowing his own daughter wasn't there to witness this significant moment? It was a thought that made me wince in discomfort.

As I looked at my dad, lost in my thoughts, he caught my eyes and offered a soft smile. It was a smile that suggested that he was happy things were going somewhat smoothly.

The loaded questions escaped my lips before I could think twice. 'So, what was the wedding like?' I blurted out, my curiosity overcoming the cautious silence that lingered between bites.

Dad paused, his fork mid-air, and exchanged a quick glance with Folake. I could sense their hesitation, the unspoken acknowledgment that certain doors were about to break open.

Folake, ever graceful, responded with a soft smile, 'It was a beautiful ceremony, we wanted to keep it very simple, so it was held in my parents' courtyard.' She glanced at Dad, her eyes shimmering with a hint of warmth.

I nodded, urging them to continue. My need to fill the gaps in my understanding outweighed the awkwardness of the conversation.

Dad cleared his throat. 'It was a small affair, we didn't invite too many people ...' His eyes held a mixture of regret and apology.

I nodded again, absorbing the details. The mental picture I had been forming began to take shape. 'So, you were really in a rush to get married?'

'Sometimes life nudges you to make decisions sooner than expected, being married on paper made a lot of things a bit easier for us when it came to travel, healthcare and legal documents, does that make sense?' Folake explained.

I nodded, absorbing their explanations. As we continued to eat, the air lightened a bit.

'So, when are you having the baby?' I asked next.

Folake practically choked on her food, but politely wiped her mouth with the tissue by her plate.

'Well, the baby is due in about four months,' she replied, drawing out each word. Her hand reached out to Dad and he held it in his.

'Are you going to live here?' I asked next, thinking about how her, my dad, a baby and Oba could even fit in her small bungalow. I doubted they'd even have room for me if I came to visit.

'She is, but don't worry, your room will stay the same,' Dad answered.

'And do you have a name yet?' I asked them, genuinely curious.

'Funny you should ask. I've been thinking about that a lot since I recently found out I'll be having a boy,' Folake said, looking excitedly at Dad. 'I'd like to call him Adedeji, it means "the crown has become two" in Yoruba.'

Dad looked at Folake with so much pride and joy in his eyes.

I had a warm feeling in my chest too, I realised I was actually happy for them. Like, for real. Adedeji – the crown has become two. It was a beautiful name, and it felt like a symbol of their new journey as a family.

'That's a wonderful name,' I said sincerely. 'It's really meaningful.'

Folake's smile widened, and I could see the relief in her eyes that I was accepting the idea more openly. 'Thank you, Abi. I'm glad you like it.'

The tension that had been lingering began to ease as we continued talking about their plans for the baby. Folake admitted she wished her family was with her during this time, especially her sisters who she said made pregnancy look easy.

As we finished dinner and cleared the table together, I realised that while the situation was far from what I had expected, there was potential for something good to come out of it. Adedeji's arrival would bring a lot of joy into the house.

I decided to be bold and use the good energy in the air to make my grand announcement and reveal what I had been thinking about when it came to my own next steps.

'Dad ... I don't think I want to study nursing,' I confessed, letting my words sink in.

Dad looked at me, struggling not to lose his cool, especially in front of Folake. 'It's a bit late to change your mind ... you've already sent off your college choices,' he said.

I took a deep breath, gathering my strength before explaining. 'I've been thinking a lot, and I've realised that I'm not passionate about nursing. I was only going with it to make you happy. When I first talked to Folake while you were away, she suggested that I follow my passion and I know for sure it's not nursing.'

Admittedly what I was doing was a bit cheeky, roping Folake in like that, but whatever works, right?

Dad's eyebrows shot up in surprise at my mention of Folake's name. He exchanged a quick look with her before turning his attention back to me.

'Folake suggested that?' he repeated, his tone very sceptical.

Folake cleared her throat softly, offering a guilty smile. 'Don't look at me like that, Deji, I just mentioned to your daughter that studying something she's passionate about is important. It's her future after all.'

Dad seemed to process this, but it wasn't computing with his 'good grades equal good degrees' academic type of thinking. 'And what is it that you're passionate about then?' he asked me, his voice waiting to judge.

I shifted, but was determined to try my luck. Like Folake said, it's my future after all.

'I'd love to study hair – professionally,' I admitted. 'I enjoy doing my own hair, but not just that, learning about other people's hair. I love how I can connect with people and how good it makes them feel.'

Dad's eyebrows furrowed; he was in absolute disbelief. 'Abidemi Benson, you want to be studying hair? That's a hobby, a side hustle ... not a very stable career!'

The use of my full name showed that he was serious. He was really back in his strict-Dad mode now. Did he really think that would work now? After everything?

I nodded, to show I understood his concerns, but from my face it was clear that I didn't agree with his points.

'I know it's not the typical career path, but I've been research-ing. There are so many ways into the hair and beauty industry – I can do a business degree then do an apprenticeship in a salon. I could even do both at the same time. The change of mind form is still open for three days, I can fill it out tonight. Dad, listen, one day I'd like to own a salon so nobody will ever have to feel like their hair is difficult or unmanageable,' I said.

Folake chimed in again, her tone gentle but supportive. 'Deji, if Abi is willing to work hard for it, she can make it happen.'

Dad looked between us; he was conflicted. He was absolutely torn between his worries for my future and his desires to support my dream.

'I just want what's best for you,' he said finally. 'What you're saying doesn't make sense to me … but I also want you to be happy with your own choices.'

I couldn't help but smile, relieved that he was open to my idea and for the first time in my life, I was excited and not scared about the journey ahead.

CHAPTER TWENTY- SEVEN

A NEW AGE

Folake was going to be moving in sooner than they had planned for. Dad asked me more times than I could count if I was OK with this. Even if I wasn't, I felt it was a bit silly to make them wait for me to leave for college so they could freely make the changes they needed to make to their living arrangements.

Folake told the agency she was renting from to put her bungalow back on the rental market. They were only delighted to see all the improvements she had made to the space and they had no doubt someone would snap it up in the coming days. They were so sure of this they put the listing up for twice the price and tagged it as a 'Luxury bungalow tastefully designed with modern aesthetics'.

In the meantime, I found myself watching the transformation of our home as her colourful personal belongings started to fill the space.

Dad had been going back and forth between our house and hers, helping her pack and bring things over. It surprised me how much stuff she owned. How had she ever managed to keep so much in her own small home?

One afternoon, I listened as Folake excitedly shared her ideas about the baby's room. I guessed that the only space for that would be the now-empty spare room. She talked about neutral wall paintings, a wooden cot and a play den and Dad listened eagerly.

That night, after I cleared the dinner table, Folake approached me with a warm smile. 'Abi, do you want to see something?' she asked. She'd been trying so hard to slowly bridge the gap.

I hesitated for a moment, unsure of what she intended to show me, but I nodded out of curiosity.

Folake retrieved her phone and scrolled through a few pictures before stopping on one. She turned the screen towards me, revealing an image. The delicate features of a tiny human form were visible, I had never seen one before, but I knew this was an ultrasound, this was the baby boy growing in her belly.

'How does that even happen?' I murmured, more to myself than to anyone in particular.

Folake chuckled gently. 'It's pretty amazing, isn't it?'

I nodded, a sense of connection forming in that shared moment. 'Thanks for showing me,' I replied, and I really did mean it.

Hearing a dog barking was something I didn't realise would take time to get used to. Oba seemed to take to the house very quickly. I watched as he explored every nook and cranny, his tail wagging with excitement as he sniffed around. What Oba truly fell in love with though was the outdoor space. Our backyard soon became his personal playground.

With so much going on around me, I had my own things to focus on. I would only be here for another month before moving to Dublin.

As the night wore on and darkness settled around me, I couldn't shake the anticipation building inside me.

Tomorrow was the first of August – the day I would officially turn eighteen.

I would be an adult in the eyes of the law and a woman in the eyes of society. All my decisions would be my own and I could take on the world.

Lying in bed, I stared at the ceiling, waiting for the clock to strike midnight. It was as if time itself had slowed down, each passing second stretching out in front of me.

The air in my room felt charged, as though the universe was lending me a moment of its magic.

My phone alarm vibrated, forcing the realisation to sink in. I closed my eyes and took a deep breath, finding comfort in the quiet of the night.

'Hello, eighteen,' I whispered to myself. 'Things are never going to be the same again.'

CHAPTER TWENTY- EIGHT

BIRTHDAY GIRL

I waited outside of Vinny's for Sinéad. Even though she was late for the special birthday lunch she had promised to take me on, she texted warning me not to come looking for her at the launderette.

I found it puzzling that she specifically instructed me to wait outside of Vinny's instead of joining the growing crowd inside. I decided not to press her for answers. I was super-excited to see Sinéad and was even more thrilled for the special birthday treatment.

The day had started off on a sweet note. Folake and Dad delivered a delicious breakfast tray to me in bed. On it was a stack of fluffy pancakes, scrambled eggs, fresh fruit and creamy yoghurt.

A 'Happy Eighteenth Birthday' card was propped up on the tray too. In it was a handwritten note full of warm wishes from both of them. The stand-out gift was of course from Dad – a stunning gold necklace with a heart-shaped pendant that sparkled with each movement. He even helped me clasp it around my neck.

Embracing my happy mood, I decided to get dressed up for the day. I put on a full face of makeup and slipped into a summery yellow dress, completing the look with the dangly earrings I'd bought from 'Thrills and Frills'. I also wore one of the chunky bracelets I had kept from Mom's belongings.

Sinéad appeared down the street, practically skipping in my direction, her tote bag bouncing across her body.

'Happy birthday, babe!' she shouted, pulling me into a warm hug and planting a kiss on my cheek.

I took in Sinéad's dramatic new look – her hair was now a deep cherry red, styled in layers that framed her face.

'You look stunning!' I exclaimed, admiring the unexpected transformation.

She playfully twirled around, highlighting her new hair. 'I feel it too!' she laughed. 'Things have been looking up at the shop, so there's some extra cash to play around with,' she said proudly. 'Ready for your special birthday lunch?' she asked, linking her arm with mine.

'Absolutely, let's head in,' I replied, expecting us to enter Vinny's for our meal.

Sinéad burst into laughter. 'Abidemi Benson, did you really think I'd drag you in here for some greasy chips on your eighteenth birthday?'

'Oh,' was all I could muster.

'We're going for a little picnic by the waterfall,' Sinéad announced, gesturing toward her bag. 'And we're going to have the longest catch-up ever. I've missed you so much.'

The stream of water pouring down into the river and the birds delicately singing in the air provided the perfect back-drop for our conversation.

Sinéad spread out a small blanket and on it she arranged a spread of homemade ham sandwiches, juicy grapes, cheese squares, chocolate bars, Fanta cans and a bag of sweet and salty popcorn.

'A feast for queens,' she said, admiring her selection and as we ate, we took in the enchanting scene around us.

A few minutes later, Sinéad opened up the conversation about the more dramatic aspects of my life. 'So, spill it, Abi. How's life with your dad's lover under the same roof?'

I knew she would bring it up, especially because I had only given her brief summaries when she'd called to ask how I was doing. I didn't want to say too much on the phone in case there were lingering ears outside my door in what was now a full house.

'It's weirdly been OK. Strangely, Folake has managed to fit right in and she's very calming to have around,' I said, deep in thought about the last few days.

Sinéad leaned in, her eyes gleaming with curiosity. 'But do you think you'll end up being close with her?'

'Maybe with time. Right now, I'm just relieved that things aren't awkward,' I admitted. 'She said it's going to be a boy, you know …' I knew that would get Sinéad even more interested.

'A boy, huh?' Sinéad's eyes widened with intrigue. 'Who knows, maybe having a little brother will be fun. You can teach him the ropes and annoy him like only an older sister can. Margaret and Deirdre sure seem to love doing that to me.'

I chuckled, considering the thought.

'Props to you for handling it maturely though,' Sinéad said, a glint of mischief in her eyes. 'If it were me, I'd probably still be angry as hell.'

I laughed at this. 'That's a lie, Sinéad, you're the most understanding person I know.'

She grinned back at me with a twinkle in her eye. 'Well, speaking of drama, secrets and scandal. I've got news too …' she said, leaning in as if she was preparing for a big reveal.

'I had a talk with Mom about art college,' Sinéad began, excitement bubbling in her voice. 'And get this – she was shocked that I have any artistic talent! Can you believe that woman? After all the posters I've made for the shop over the years.'

I laughed along with her, encouraging her to continue.

'Anyway, I showed her my art portfolio and confessed that I missed out on this year's scholarship round, but that I could try again next year ...' Sinéad paused, waiting for the silence to create some dramatic effect, 'and guess what? Mom was totally supportive! Well, she actually called me an idiot for not coming to her sooner ... same thing though.'

'That's fantastic!' I exclaimed, genuinely happy for her. If Sinéad did go to college next year, that would make her the first person in her family to pursue higher education.

Sinéad beamed, her excitement contagious. 'I know, right? I was so nervous, thinking she'd pull out the "you need a real job" lecture. But no, she was surprisingly cool about it. It's like I don't even know her anymore.'

It struck me that this was a milestone, a step towards a future her family might not have envisioned. I couldn't shake the contrast between Sinéad's school experience and mine. In my home, the expectation to go to college had always been a given. Dad encouraged my educational pursuits without a second thought.

I found myself contemplating the privileges I had taken

for granted. The stability, the support, and the assumption that opportunities for education were readily available – all of these had been constants. Sinéad, on the other hand, was breaking new ground with financial uncertainties ahead of her.

I felt a twinge of guilt for the ways I subtly made Sinéad feel bad for not being as invested in school as I was. If the roles were reversed, I probably would have treated school in the exact same nonchalant way she had.

'I can't believe I thought you were simply avoiding me after the disco – you've had so much to work through. I'm sorry if I haven't been understanding …' I admitted to Sinéad. I wanted to make amends and let her know I cared about our friendship, a lot.

'Trust me, I loved being in that big old house while your dad was away and it hurt me not to talk to you for what was it, like, three whole days,' Sinéad said, 'but after the disco, something just switched in me. I just needed to be alone and clear my head properly. So, you're not wrong, I was kind of being weird for a bit there.'

I was about to lean in to hug her, but just then, my phone buzzed. It was a text from Dad which simply read, 'Be home by four, please.'

No pleasantries or anything.

Was there an emergency? Did something happen?

What could be so serious, I thought to myself while trying not to panic.

I showed the message to Sinéad, who immediately began packing up the leftovers of our picnic.

'Looks like we've got to go,' she said, a hint of concern in her tone. 'We should hurry.'

CHAPTER TWENTY- NINE

PURE JOY

As we pushed open the front door, the house was unusually silent.

Dad's message had seemed urgent, but there was no sign of him or Folake even though both their cars were still parked out front. I checked the kitchen and the garden; Oba wasn't there either.

Could they have gone for a walk? If so, why would they ask me to come back here?

Sinéad shot me a questioning look, her eyebrows raised in curiosity. 'Where is everyone?' she whispered.

'I have no idea,' I replied, just as baffled.

We exchanged puzzled looks and then walked down the hallway toward the living room. The door was closed. Strange!

My heart started racing as I reached for the doorknob. I

turned it slowly, pushing the door open inch by inch. The curtains were drawn, and the room was dark.

'SURPRISE!'

The greeting was so loud it nearly knocked me off my feet.

Someone drew the curtains open; the living room was absolutely covered with balloons and over the fireplace was a sparkling banner held up with curly ribbons. My eyes darted around, taking it all in. In the corner was a table with a large blue birthday cake, cupcakes, sausage rolls, crisps, and an array of sweet treats.

Dad stood there, a huge grin on his face. Folake, too, her eyes beaming with joy. Then I saw him – Jack, wearing a casual smile that told me he was clearly in on this too.

Wait! It seemed everyone was here.

Vinny from the chipper. All the Quinns: Sinéad's sisters and even her mam. Everyone was watching me come to the realisation that this was a surprise party. For me!

Anne, who looked the most dressed up I'd ever seen her, seemed delighted with herself. She and Ms Kelly wore paper party hats, the kind you see at children's parties.

Then a pair of eyes met mine and I froze. Clara and her mom were also here, standing by the window. Clara's mom looked slightly confused about what was going on and Clara just looked happy to be here.

Then there were even more faces that I was surprised to see: the Callaghan brothers, Niamh, Shauna, Marie-Clare as well as some other friends from St Enda's.

Dad was the first to reach out to me, pulling me into a tight hug.

'Happy eighteenth birthday, my daughter,' he whispered, his voice full of affection.

Tears stung my eyes, threatening to spill out.

Don't ruin your makeup, Abi, I thought to myself, thankful that I had dressed up for the day.

Sinéad was now giggling beside me and clapping her hands.

I turned to her. 'You *knew* about this?' I asked.

Sinéad's grin widened. 'Of *course*, Abi! It was my idea, after all. Did you really think I'd let your eighteenth birthday pass by without a proper celebration?'

'You basically invited half of our year,' I said.

'I even made up with the three – sorry, I'm trying to be a better person. I texted Clara, Niamh and Shauna about this party, which as you can imagine wasn't easy for me,' Sinéad said mischievously.

I was completely overwhelmed by the love and effort that had gone into this surprise. As the group started singing 'Happy Birthday', my dad moved toward the cake. He lit the sparklers and candles, and the chorus of voices pulled me into their centre.

It was time for me to make a wish.

I closed my eyes, the happy faces of those I loved flashing before me. The world seemed to blur as I considered what to wish for. The truth was my mind drew a blank. There was so much pure joy and pure love already surrounding me. All I wanted was for this feeling to last forever.

With my heart full, I exhaled softly, blowing out the burning candles. The room erupted in cheers and applause and this time it was Ms Kelly who reached out to hug me, followed by Clara.

'You look stunning, babe. Happy birthday,' Clara whispered into my ear.

As the celebration continued and my classmates started to show off their dance moves in the centre of the room, I found myself drawn to the window. I stared up to the heavens where the sun was now starting to set.

I closed my eyes and hoped that my mom, wherever she was, could see just how far I had come, how much I had grown, and how much I was loved. I turned back to the room, with a heart full of gratitude, and there stood Jack, holding a card in his hand.

The card was unmistakably Sinéad's work – a playful portrayal of a girl with braids, surrounded not by a halo of confetti, which was my first thought, but by golden chips raining down upon her. I couldn't help but burst into laughter at the creative humour.

The card's message read: *Vinny and I didn't know what to bring, so we're offering something we know you'll accept – a lifetime of free chips. Consider this card your infinite token.'*

It was a hilarious and incredibly thoughtful gift that perfectly captured my teenage days.

'I love it so much, thank you,' I said, wrapping my arms around Jack who looked pleased with himself.

'I'm glad you like it! We brainstormed for a while to come up with something fun,' Jack said.

After some more laughter and chatter, Jack leaned in and lowered his voice. 'By the way, Abi, Vinny was talking to your dad, and I hear that you're considering the business school in Dublin?'

I blinked in surprise. 'Yeah, I'm hoping to get in,' I replied, wondering why this topic was coming up now.

With a playful grin, Jack continued, 'Well, that's *very* interesting because I'm hoping to do the same.'

My heart skipped a beat as his words sank in. Did that mean – Jack and I were both looking at going to the same business school? It made sense that that was what he was interested in after all the years spent behind the till at Vinny's. A warm feeling of excitement bubbled within me, and a smile spread across my face.

'So, what you're saying is that I might still be seeing you around – even after you take me out on that pasta date you talked about?' I asked. I had been looking for a way to casually let him know I was ready, more than ready even, eager to be around him as much as possible before the summer ended.

Every time I tried to write the text, the butterflies in my tummy would make me blush and delete my cringey words.

Jack laughed, his eyes crinkling at the corners. 'I can be free anytime you're free,' he said.

'Well, you're in luck Jack Keane, I'm basically free every-day till September,' I teased, the playfulness in my tone concealing the subtle excitement bubbling within me. The anticipation of what he would say next made my heart race.

Jack was now doing that thing where he looked at me in a way that made my palms sweaty, and my knees turn to jelly. 'How about tomorrow?' he asked.

I looked to the crowd to see if my dad was watching, but he and Folake looked to be deep in conversation with Clara's mom. Maybe it was all the bravery that came with turning eighteen, but I wanted to show Jack that he wasn't the only one that had the ability to charm.

OK, so I didn't actually know if I had the ability to charm, but I had certainly learnt a thing or two from the romantic films I've coincidentally been watching over the last few days.

I leaned in closer to Jack and wrapped my arms around his neck and he instinctively wrapped his around my waist.

'Does this answer your question?' I asked, pressing my lips against his. Jack responded to the kiss by gently pulling me closer.

After what felt like both an eternity and a fleeting second, we reluctantly pulled away, our eyes meeting in shared surprise and delight. A shy smile played on Jack's lips, mirroring the unspoken understanding between us.

'You're full of surprises, Abi,' he chuckled, a warmth in his eyes that made my heart flutter.

Before I could respond with something smart, a voice rang out, breaking the moment.

'Hey, lovebirds ... get in!' Sinéad's voice called out. I looked over Jack's shoulder and there she was waving for us to come over.

Sinéad had been directing everyone to pose for a group picture and we were the only two missing. The corners of my lips curled up as I shared a knowing look with Jack.

'Say "cheese"!' Sinéad called out, leaving her phone propped up against a cup on the table. She ran towards the group and so did we, making it just in time for the ten-second countdown.

The camera flashed and clicked, sealing this moment in time.

One day, I will look back at this and remember the sense of belonging. Each person here representing a small piece of the puzzle that makes me who I am.

As I stood there, laughing with family and friends, I realised I truly felt ready to embrace the future.

The journey into the unknown awaited and I had everything I needed to face whatever lay ahead.

ACKNOWLEDGEMENTS

ACKNOWLEDGEMENTS

Stories have always been intricately linked to the core of my being. From a young age, I realised that, regardless of life's twists and turns, the act of storytelling – whether rooted in fact or fiction – would be necessary for my personal growth. I hold the belief that every storyteller is a product of seeds sown by others, and under the right conditions, their penned words can be heard and shared globally. I am thankful for my small but mighty community of people who have watered me from the very beginning. My parents, siblings, partner, and friends have not only graciously entertained my ideas but have also propelled me forward with delight and enthusiasm. I am grateful for the ways in which they've never constrained my dreams, no matter how grand and wild they may seem at times. I also want to thank author and children's books champion, Sarah Webb. Little did she know that she would serve as a catalyst, leading me to the brilliant team at the O'Brien Press. To those who believed in my initial draft of *Braids Take A Day*, your faith and encouragement will forever hold a special place in my heart. Thank you for showing this book so much love and allowing it to hold weight even before we all knew that it would one day take up space on bookshelves.

TURN THE PAGE FOR MORE
GREAT BOOKS FROM
THE O'BRIEN PRESS

Freya Harte is Not a Puzzle

Freya's always felt different, so when she learns she's autistic she doesn't want anyone to know. All she wants is to fit in. But does she really need to change herself or can she find friends who like her just the way she is? A novel about friendship, discovering who you really are – and being OK with that!

FINDING A VOICE
FRIENDSHIP IS A TWO WAY STREET ...
KIM HOOD

Shortlisted for the YA Book Prize

Finding a Voice

Jo can't tell anyone how hard it is living with her
mentally ill mother. Chris literally has no way to
speak at all. Together, can they
finally find their voices?